COME,
THE RESTORER

By *William Goyen*

COME,
THE RESTORER

A NOVEL BY

William Goyen

DOUBLEDAY & COMPANY, INC.

GARDEN CITY, NEW YORK   1974

Grateful acknowledgment is made to *The Southwest Review* and *Transatlantic Review* for their permission to print the portions of this novel that have already appeared in their pages.

Library of Congress Cataloging in Publication Data
Goyen, William.
    Come, the restorer.

    I. Title.
PZ3.G7484Co   813'.5'4
ISBN 0-385-00767-1
Library of Congress Catalog Card Number 74–2829

1814231

For *Doris*
and in memory of *Ann*

Contents

Lost
Rose

Few people know—and they cannot tell—what went into the making of one rich American city.

The city of Rose, Texas is one of the largest and richest in America. Its refineries, its chemical plants, its technological wonderworks have enriched and enlarged it beyond the statistics of most American cities; and municipal wealth has wound about it like a spool Expressways, Throughways, Freeways and Clover-leafs. Once it was (supposedly) and to the naked eye just a plain town near the Thicket and near the Gulf, a filled-in swampland of frame houses with the smell of natural gas hanging over it.

Yet few people know what went into the making of Rose. There has never been a true chronicle of the city, for that would be impossible: no one is available who knows what went on underneath the spectacular growth of that city from its humble and prosaic beginnings. Those who could tell have mysteriously vanished, or are dead and buried, or are not of reliable memory—not what you'd call dependable historians. What follows is, perhaps, a chronicle of Rose—the Rose Saga, perhaps. The point is, you only see the visible Rose, you do not see the lost.

Important to the rise and financial splendor of Rose is the figure of Wylie Prescott—among other figures of sleep,

death, resurrection, beauty, and power who were the ances-
tors and forebears of Rose. Wylie Prescott was the leader of
that generation that made poison and that ate its own poison;
that cemented over land and grass; that built shopping centers;
a man of greed and vulgarity who provided an inheritance of
magic. Now how could this be? People often wonder how
Wylie Prescott was able to make such a bequeathment to a
posterity for which he was a pioneer creator of ugliness and
death.

Wylie Prescott's uncle was Ace Adair, his aunt was Jewel
Adair. They lived in an old house built by Jewel's grandparents. Jewel and Ace Adair's adopted son was Wylie's
"cousin"—Addis Adair, vanished since he was fifteen but
always expected back. For many years, one of Wylie's fears
was that "cousin" Addis Adair would suddenly reappear and
claim inheritance, an anxiety which diminished as the years
passed and Addis Adair, always expected, never came.

And Mr. de Persia! Elite repairman in an age of breakdown!
Ah, if he'd come back and build the world again. Mr. de
Persia! people of Rose cried out, who gave us back the world,
can the world not give you back to us? Guess not. The world
takes everything away, get used to it.

But about Mr. de Persia, when the world was young in
Rose . . .

Part I

THE TIMES OF
MR. DE PERSIA

1
Come, The
Restorer

Come a restorer to us, out of the Panhandle, in those days. Come back!

His name was Mr. de Persia. Gave us no first name as long as we knew him, which is everybody's lifetime. 'd been coming here that long in everybody's memory, going through the towns rescuing from fading photos the faces of those passed away and gone, or brightening the dimming features of those still here. When he came around he brought back a company of lost people, all before us risen up out of our shoeboxes and cedarchests like ghosts out of their graves. Mr. de Persia resurrected half our town and brought back old times, reviving the dead and renewing the perishing with his magic sleight-of-hand (as he called it). Restorer! Creator and re-creator, come back!

If he'd come back now, if he'd come back, man of salvations, I'd bring him first that old photo of Ace Adair, so handsome in his striped railroad overalls and in his Switchman's cap, a photo made so long ago that 'tis hardly of him any more, so shadowy and melting away, like something's drawing him into the darkness. I want Ace restored out of the darkness. Looking for that old photo of Ace in the goodsbox I come upon a whole lot of his things all put away, pore Ace's sad things: looked for his Switchman's cap that'd hung out on the back porch on that same nail's been out there all these years; but couldn't find it, don't know why. But found his Hamilton railroad watch, found that, and put it in my pocket. That old thing runs smart as ever, face of it still pure white and the big pretty numbers shining black. Pore Ace, time goes on on his railroad watch but he's gone. Bring him back a little in his photo, Mr. de Persia.

And I'd take the restorer one of Jewel Adair. Save her Mr. de Persia, I'd implore. It 'tis a once-tinted picture of her with a piece of blue voile draped across her breasts, then so live and sensitive-looking must have been a pain to have them on her, like thorns in her bosom, at age of 16, in the year her womanhood took hold of her and she looked in a kind of a glory and so afraid. Jewel Adair is rinsed of almost all color—can you bring back the original tint?—the voile looks almost like a funeral shroud, 'tis gray upon her breasts. And feet of some creature have scarred Jewel Adair like age around the mouth and eyes, once blue; can you take out scratches of something that got at her photo where it lay in the goodsbox, scratching mice or some clawing little something that got in the goodsbox? didn't seem right to put a trap or poison among the photographs. Of course could've been mildew; mildew can eat at something as if it had teeth and leave a scar—mold is as bad as a living varmint, Lord Jesus I hate mold that rots.

And oh I'd bring the restorer one of Ace Adair and Jewel, sitting on the front porch steps. Some smoke, some cloud, some kind of a gloom is coming in over that photo and overwhelming it, creeping in over the picture from behind Ace and Jewel Adair like a soft storm, a gray fog: restore them, Mr. de Persia: bring that back.

And one more I'd bring him, oh. The one where a bursting white light is exploding out from behind the well house where three figures was standing together in the backyard, Ace and Jewel and pore little Addis Adair, another man's son, so pitiful and tender, cringing up against his "mother" like a little orphan, on a chill March Sunday near Easter time, when the redbud tree was abloom. What is that bursting light? Can you take that out? If you can lighten dark then can't you darken light? And oh that tree! that tree that always bloomed for Easter, oh when that sweet tree was green! Before Papa burnt it, before the treedevil got it and Papa had to burn it. Can you, Mr. de Persia, salvager, can you make green again what is now dry? The webs of the treedevil are so frail and pretty at first when they are just spun out and so white as fleece. They're like a big hoop shining in the sun, as though they were hung up in a tree like an ornament. Until you look closer and see the ungodly worms inside devouring all the life of the leaves. Just you try and poke through that silken tent those treedevils make. Even a red-hot poker would hardly burn through, that silk is like an armor. I hate worms above most anything God created. Once, in a terrible hot time, with no rain for ages, Papa tried to burn out a treedevil's nest in the redbud tree with a torch, and it set the whole redbud tree on fire. A whole big burning tree! Right there, there in the photo, that very tree that's all abloom, in the years before the tree was burnt and is the stump you see back there right now. Funny way to remember somebody, isn't it? But many times when I look back there and suddenly see that old burnt stump of the redbud tree, I think of Papa and that whole big burning tree. Mr. de Persia, restore the generations, save what's lost. Oh bring back!

That's my job, he used to say. I do it with a brush, a pen, some fluid, and a secret process. That's all the magic that I use and 'tis no witchcraft (as some said). But he'd look real morbid then and like a kind of a devil, with's red eyes aburning and the tip of his red tongue between his hairy lips. The savior Mr. de Persia was bound to have had some devil in him, naturally. How could anybody with such artful hands and such a talent of the imagination not have some of the devil in him.

So come a mender to us too. Come a repairman out of the oiltown country, out of Daisetta. 'Twas—you're right—the same Mr. de Persia, in's Ford coupé, man of many miracles and royal like a king, and magical, and handsome and devilish in his dark mustache and manly figure. Repair us!

Nothing but death is unrepairable, said Mr. de Persia the repairman. Can't raise Lazarus, but can make what's dead *look* like life. They "restored" that painting in the City Hall, damaged by water, I said. They "restored" that ancient church that was destroyed by fire, I said. But can human feelings be "restored," Mr. de Persia? *Never the same, but yes!* you'd say. *But we want the same,* I'd say. Yet never again the same, once it has been broken. In a state of permanent inner disrepair. Yes, there are all the pieces back in their place. But the life between the pieces is gone, the joining life, the unseen running current of vitality that exists in wholeness is gone. There is no longer wholeness. When something is repaired, it is the wholeness of it that is not there any longer in that thing: that is gone forever. The entirety of it, the one-ness of it is shaken and leans from its foundation, it's off its center. Its core is disturbed, from which forces extend, flow out and issue; from which its vitality—egg force—horns out and beaks out, breaks through crust, like a blind chick in an egg. How to repair the disturbed egg of something? Oh, Mr. de Persia, restorer, proud repairman, can you restore or mend anything of *that?*

(And oh, big man, do not bring again to me my yokefellow my accursedness. The accursed thing in me has been there all my days. In all my memory, there, in me. What is it? Oh, how can I put it? Just a heartbreak feeling. Suffering in my mind, sadness, like oh I want to cry for all things: my yokefellow my accursedness my cross my suffering. Out of this

dark disturbance repair me, restore me. Help me *put back.*
Can anything that is hurt, taken away, displaced, broken, be
restored ever?)

So what, Mr. de Persia, can you do about it? What can you
make—or remake—of it? Is there any chance, is there any
hope? To make *like new?* Once it's broken, all you can do, I
guess, oh helpless, hopeless, most pitifully, mercifully, pro-
foundly ineffectual, hands-tied Mr. de Persia, all you can do is
try to remake it: *like new.* Repair us! Rebuild! Remake! Redeem!

And when you come, find your way across what would
otherwise be a run-of-the-mill pasture except for one pretty
thing: bubbles up shining dandelions on a very early morning.
Find your way as I have described . . . it's, well, you can ask
somebody if you can't find it . . . and come to a slanted little
one-sided leaning house, wood mouse-colored with weather
that's put a kind of a soft fur on the wood—ever noticed that?
—like wood grows a pelt to protect itself, as an animal will do
against weather.

Anyway, come to that lopsided house and inside it Lord,
God, Mr. de Persia you will find just a piece of a person. A
saint and a cunning saint. Don't try to pull a fast one on *her.*
Her eyes are like snakes that strike at you every move you
make. She lives, old Sybil, in those snaky eyes. A powerful
spirit of the Lord God inhabits that crooked house a little
piece, just a little bitty piece of humanity is breathing and
flooding out life in that slanted house. She was born one-third
of a normal person and then lost most of that—she's just a
bunch of holes—mouth, ears, nose, eyes, etc.—and a back-
bone. Mend old Sybil, Mr. de Persia. Help her to move
around. Can't you build a contraption for her? Something on
wheels: can't you invent a gadget that would move her

around, needn't be anything much lighter than a fly-swatter since Sybil is so light and easy to move, light as a fly, couldn't you make some kind of a machine that would fly her through her pore air in her little slanted house?

Mr. de Persia did you dream of mending the broken chain of life? Mr. magic mender, invisible weaver, redeemer of faded faces and scarred features, can you not mend the broken chain of life? Come back again to our place; pass by! Restore us to the days before the ugliness, to the times before Rose River was ruined by the chemical factory up at River-side, and there was good water. There in the springtime, there by Rose River, by the sweet little water, that little water running so clear, you'd have thought that nothing could ever happen to any of us that would bring us any sorrow. There was green leaves, and little tree birds. Now we have no redemption and the world is ruined. A glory's passed away from this old earth. Return!

It might be said you made a Garden of Eden here. You grafted trees and pruned and cut back and pinched back and laid your heavy hand on big trees and your light one on the shoots—strange they call them young shoots—they do shoot, don't they?—such a shooting shaft they seem, Mr. de Persia, knower of all such things. But then, in those shooting days, things were thrusting up in that light green, out of the ground just thawing, shafting up, so tender, wouldn't even touch them to bruise them but oh how strong they were going to be.

And included among the things you helped to sprout and shoot and spurt and thrust, sweet gardener, oh do you separate? I mean my bulbs, my Irises and some old Grape Hyacinths, guess, I imagine, about a century old, the Adairs must first have put them in for they are visible in early photos when the house was new. And could you, besides separating, rejuvenate the aging one by the old well house—the one in the photo shows it plainly though the picture-taker (wonder who the picture-taker was, wonder who?) got it sideways along with the well house, so could you straighten the well

house, please? The old well's in there, you know; drop a stone
in it and wait and wait to finally hear the quavering drum
sound—'s that deep a well, full of snakes 'tis said, my God
have mercy on a well of snakes. The old well house, wasn't I
saying? is aslant in the photo with the aging Grape Hyacinth.
So could you please, Mr. de Persia, set the well house upright
on its foundations, oh repairman, oh restorer.

I guess I'm asking you to come back and re-do the whole
place from hyacinth to well house. Too much repairing to be
done by one man, I guess, and in an age of breakdown, but
oh—and *very* important—my aircondition! Would you know
about those? There is a problem. The song in my music box is
broken. Come, please, Mr. de Persia, to my room and see
what can you do about my Fedders, where late the sweet
birds sang. Suddenly there was the sweetest little singing in
my Fedders, there being a spring nest there causing me not to
turn on the aircondition but to drag in the old electric fan
haven't used in years, so old couldn't even oscillate. First 'twas
the parents' song, oh so sweet: later there was the frail twit-
tering of the newborn. Every morning and every evening at
twilight I'd hear the sweet song in my window—how sweet!
How could I describe it to anyone who'd never heard that
music. Was it a cardinal? Was it a meadowlark was it an ori-
ole? In the early morning I'd sit there and listen to the song
like the meadowlarks in the days before, in the times before
the ugliness. Disturb not my song, I said, and do not turn on
the Fedders aircondition, the very first to be installed in
Rose. And then Satan himself must have mashed that ON button—I know to my soul that I did not—and oh my God my
Fedders chopped to shreds the sweet choir and ruined my
Easter song, I could just die. Haven't been able to get over it,
has hurt me so deep, the slaughter of those little birds, the
devastation of that sweet singing. Oh Mr. de Persia, *who*
mashed my ON button? song-killer, song-chopper, ruiner of
choirs! Mr. de Persia maker of precious replacements, bring
back the song!

And sir, Mr. de Persia, come to the place on the righthand side of the Mortuary and in that yellow house (used to be yellow, now a grayish color but town still refers to it as the yellow house) find an old deaf son-of-a-bitch shut-in, mean as the Devil incarnate, name's Shot (short for Schotke, German man, been here for sixty years, baker—Schotke's Bakery: the town's intestines are caked with the putty he called bread and sold to us for fifty years, what part of local humanity's innards not caked with Shot's putty is dyed with Wylie Prescott's chemicals in our drinking water, that scoundrel ought to hold him down and dye his you-know-what is what I say: anyway Shot Schotke lived for fifty years with a woman (not his wife) that we only knew as Aunt Lou, died from falling down the cellar, don't ask me why or anything more because I honest-to-God don't know—nor do I care). Old Shot needs to hear something. Aren't there inventions now for that? Couldn't you imagine something, fixer that you are, to stick into an old man's ear to help him hear something?

Once you traced the door panes of our houses with frosted figures of knights on prancing steeds with flowing silvery manes. Made our weather vanes of cocks and owls, foxes and doves, arrows and Cupids and some say the organs of love though they were plainly fruits. Mr. de Persia of two hands, lighthanded and heavyhanded, one hand fleet and light, the other heavy and dark, wizard repairman of two stranger hands, you were just short of being a god. So get up and come back from wherever you, too, have vanished to. With your fleet hand you enameled, you laid in semiprecious stones, you crystallized, you filigreed, you silvered mirrors. With your delicate long-fingered one, of aerial workings like a spider, you touched the wrists, earlobes, necks and fingers of women with shining ornaments of gold, silver and glass, and you left behind, rusting in attics of old houses or dusty in toyboxes of vanished children, in cedarchests and jewelboxes, tarnishing in junk shops, antique shops and pawn shops, your magnificent and semidivine handiwork. Touch our town again with your faery hand that touched gables, newels, woodwork of empty hallways, ceilings, mantels, fireplaces and mirrors of darkened and falling houses. Rot and decay are there, eating at your magical trace that lingers after you, our houses rot and fall. Builder come back, rebuild!

With your dark and heavy hand, hairy and sexual—this was the pounding one—you shod iron on the hooves of horses, set iron eyes in woodstoves, forged shares for plows. But with your light hand you inscribed, as frail as frost, on a plowshare: *an ox and an ass must not pull the same plow* (*Deut.*). And I have seen traced on a lavaliere that was somebody's precious gift, in the finest hand, as if a dragonfly had worked it:

> *Have you seen a bright lily grow*
> *Before rude hands have touched it?*

And on a grain shovel made of copper: *Better is an handful with quietness, than both the hands full, with travail and vexation of spirit.* (*Eccles. 4:6*).

Rise up and return now, to what is dying and fading and rotting and falling to one side; oh Mr. de Persia, wonderman, restore us our days gone by.

But Mr. de Persia didn't come. So many people expected that never come—that's life. My tale begins. I half shudder to tell it. Read on and you will see.

2

Restore
The Restorer

'Twas said that this cocked-gun sleep in which Mr. de Persia dwelt had been devised by some witch that had enchained him in bonds of sleep forever. He was encasketed in a tub of glass, his heavy hand holding his light hand cupped tenderly in it as though it were something it had just scooped up out of water. The watery casket of Mr. de Persia was a deep, wide bathtub made of thick icelike glass, a creation of Mr. de Persia for his own pleasure? for sale? on capricious commission from somebody who never came back for it? Whatever the reason, Mr. de Persia made it and one morning was found deeply asleep in it in the rear of his workshop. Possibly a swindler named Craig Corinth, lumber king, cotton king, oil king, etc., had asked Mr. de Persia to make a tub deep as a pool like this one for his lascivious bathroom in the mansion which he had suddenly so mysteriously abandoned, disappearing in the East. It was rumored that Craig Corinth had a special liking for bathtubs, and not a few girls of the town had been his guests in his marble one and reports held it to be a sensational experience. Whatever the reason or why ever he had made it, Mr. de Persia one morning was found deeply asleep in it, and in full erection.

Mr. de Persia lay in his full length and splendor asleep in some swoon. At first, people stood back from him as if he were holding a gun on them. But soon they came closer. Being a man of godlike accomplishment, he would sometimes go a little off his rocker (drank a little, too) and would chase a woman like a fox after a hen; sleight-of-hand, too—he was so sleight that he could get fingers playing on you like a harmonica, up your leg before you knew it. Whether it was true or superstition in a back town in the 1920s in East Texas on the edge of The Big Thicket wilderness, it was said that Mr. de Persia, being a magician and adept at magic spells, had taught someone how to cast a certain spell of life-invigorating sleep—it might have been just a joke or trick, who knew?— but hadn't time to divulge the magic way to break the spell before that person, the student, had tried it out on *him*, the teacher, and Lord God, it worked; and there lay Mr. de Persia enchanter enchanted by his own enchantment.

So here lay the sovereign Mr. de Persia dressed in his purple silken suit made of Italian goods in his glass casket, asleep under his own spell. Who could raise him up, this attractive body sprawled out with penile erection tenting up his purple silk? Who could restore the restorer? Mrs. Hand, the legal secretary, was brought in at once to notarize the discovery. Why? Don't ask me. She stood back from him as if he were holding a gun on her. She suggested that flowers or a flag be placed upon Mr. de Persia's "privacy." It was from Mrs. Hand's mouth that word issued over the town that bright morning and the whole town rushed to regard the striking figure of the wizard and elite Mr. de Persia in a trance and with a massive hard-on.

Had Mr. de Persia, craftsman that he was, devised this cask of glass for his own pleasure? It was shaped like a chest and the glass was of pure unscarred clarity, except for a few bubbles in it that gave it a starry quality and made it seem buoyant, as if afloat on little balloons. The glass had a musclelike substance here and there—it was a coarse, sinewy but rich deep glass of a leaden texture and in the sunlight it blazed up in a yellow molten glow or was absolutely white and blinding. At night it became a dark blue frozen color. What a beautiful and odd creation for Mr. de Persia! of pure lightness, gaiety, and sensuality. What devilish mischief led the enchanter to so bedaze Mr. de Persia—and dressed like that—was the riddle of the community. He lay like something of Creation, transcendent, this maker—awful and almighty and seeming to be of the foundations, of the fundament, basic, like the solid glass, though light as air and very fleshly. His purple silk suit was skin-tight and showed him to be a cut of well-formed proportion. His persistently erect member baffled local medical authorities (if you could call Dr. Percy Searles an authority—or even medical—he was just local was about all you could say about *him*, considering the outrageous mistaken diagnosis he'd made on the community). Dr. Searles had "palpated" (means feel of) the organs of half the town and was simply waiting around for the other half to fill out enough to present him something to get hold of—male *and* female; so guess you could call him *something* of an authority on *that*.

Various questions continued to arise and several incidents worth reporting. But some of the immediate questions were concerned with who was to guard or stand by the body of Mr. de Persia lying there like an unslung slingshot until the spell upon him could be broken or would break itself. A vicious hound? A trusty from the pen? Someone suggested three nuns from Sacred Heart Convent, and so forth.

But nothing was done. And then two young Texas Rangers were assigned to the guarding of Mr. de Persia. Soon they'd need the Militia, though, because people were jammed in the one-story building that was Mr. de Persia's shop, standing out in the yard, and some were even up on the roof.

And then, right off, a man who said he was a distant cousin of Mr. de Persia's announced by telegraph at the railroad station the fact of his existence in Chattanooga, Tennessee, and that he knew a secret that would no doubt solve the riddle of

the sleeper. He signed his name Clarence Custanza; and
Clarence Custanza arrived, proclaiming that he was of Spanish descent.

He was dressed, to be blunt, like a pimp. If you think I'm
exaggerating, have you ever seen a man wear *silver* shoes?
But mystics dress odd and he was the leader of a group called
Outré with its home office (the "mother" he called it) in Chattanooga, but far flung in its reach and influence. He worked
over his distant cousin half the night, changing headdresses
several times (one looked exactly like a woman's Easter hat—
we should have known *then*) and cooing foreign-sounding
words in fogs of incense; there were torches, too, and a rooster
head—and always Clarence Custanza's silver shoes. By dawn
he had failed miserably and would have been driven out of
town *then*, simply on the basis of his outrageousness if not for
his several offenses of petty thievery and feeling up girls, but
he was tolerated in good spirit—'twas not a bad town really—
for Clarence Custanza (of Spanish descent) from Chattanooga, Tennessee, and National President of *Outré*, was of no
durable harm and, in reality, quite a dear buffoon, once you
got to know him. And anyway he was abruptly summoned
back to Chattanooga by his organization, due to an emer-
gency.

It was the third day and Mr. de Persia, straining his Italian
suit, slept on. Others wrote or came. Some sent elixirs, potions,
keys, codes, voodoo stuff. Some mailed in crackpot instruc-
tions and incantations. A dancing Indian appeared, in full
feather and bell, and danced, no one was sure quite why, but
it was colorful. Mr. de Persia slept on. And a ratty little man
materialized saying he was the second coming of Jesus—but
we'd had so many of *those* before that he was ignored and so
preached to empty street corners and did not resurrect the
sleeper.

Then who would come and rehabilitate the sleeping maker,
lying dozing in his force, his making powers ready and

primed but lying, drawn like an arrow taut in the bow, un-
shot; like a volley stuffing a cannon, straining to be shot; a
stone heavy in the loaded sling, pulled back and trembling to
be cast out, chamber loaded, cocked, reared back to spurt out
issue, to shoot out sons, Mr. de Persia had no *mind* to do it,
only the dumb instrument, like a brute upraised hammer; his
making spirit was unaware and stupid in sleep; he was just
pure dreamless instinct.

The town quite swelled, like Mr. de Persia, and prospered,
and, in truth, had never been so excited. Yet, with all this, Mr.
de Persia lay serene and hard as a rock. Naturally, thousands
stood in line to view Mr. de Persia. Had a King died? A Ma-
hatma? A God?

Yet it was known that Mr. de Persia was impotent. The
great maker could no longer get it up. He had made a point
of his condition. He had advertised—first asking for any kind
of suggestion of a remedy—and, my Lord, he got all kinds.
Then he reversed his state of mind, his attitude towards his
condition and proclaimed, like an evangelist, the beauty and
glory of chastity—*enforced* chastity, that is. For such a brawny
and well-built man (as half that part of the country could
now attest to), so obviously sensual and craving sexual delight, you'd have thought he suffered immensely. But he
seemed full of renunciation. Yet here was the avowedly impotent Mr. de Persia with all his glory restored—in full flag
unfurled, in gorgeous bloom, or as the farmers would say, in
full ear and pod.

Priapism. Here was a word you'd have thought would
never in the history of this town be uttered or found use for,
need even to be written, much less spoken. Yet a doctor of
note from New York, upon reading of the incident of Mr. de
Persia, hurled into town this odd word to describe the condition of Mr. de Persia. He sent a brief article explaining that
Priapus was a God of ancient times. The article explained to
the town that Mr. de Persia was suffering from "Priapism",

which meant unrelenting erection of the penis. Certain figures
had been used in olden days and ancient times as fertility
figures—people worshiped these *phalluses,* another word this
New York doctor thrust into the town's midst. "He means
Mr. de Persia's peter," old Shot, the bakery owner, said. "A
what this doctor called *phallus* is just a highfalutin word for
your *dick.*"

Well, this article troubled the town. Certain women who
were barren naturally appeared and loitered around the
sleeper in the chest of glass but—most interesting—certain
men, studs from their mouth only, hung around, too. One was
caught exposing his *phallus* to the sleeper, hoping for his lost
power to be restored. And he maintained a reputation of
supercocksman of the locale. Well, people appreciated his
honesty and pitied his problem. So for others. If the purpose
of the spell, if "Priapism" was the reason to get put into such a
sleep, if it was the handiwork of the Enchanter, half a county
would have organized a posse, old and young, to hunt down
and capture the priceless magician. Yet the other half said,
"Forget it. What good is Priapism if a spell of sleep goes with
it? You might last as long as the Flood, but you wouldn't
know or feel a thing." But it would be doing a fine service to
others, some protested. And, besides, who knew whether the
sleep was so unknowing and unfeeling? You might have a hell
of a time, and never be exhausted, never spent. It is something to think of—that if the Charmer were found she could
become a rich person, cause a revolution in lovemaking, be
sought after over the world.

So you see the town changed because of the sleeping hero
in the glass tub. Compassion, mercy, openness came over the
town. There were reconciliations, forgiveness. There was also
one hell of a renaissance of lovemaking. The town, like Mr.
de Persia (excepting of course the unfortunates I've mentioned) was one big orgy. They went to it morning, noon and
night. I mean it was a fucking town, alive, happy, vital—and

peaceful: there was neither time for fights nor energy, not even any desire to quarrel or fume around over this or that. In fact, the population became so hot, so horny and insatiable that there was an electricity over the place you could light it with. Mr. de Persia had brought such lust over everybody that not much work was done. Used in another way the libidinous ferocity of the town could have caused a revolution. 'Twas real scary. And yet the best time everybody had ever had in the history of the town. The fact is that the town was bouncing and pounding and grinding so extensively that a sort of natural holiday occurred, without proclamation, because the stores were practically empty; so everything was just voluntarily shut down and everybody went to it, old and young. It was believed that there was not a virgin left excepting perhaps Mrs. Hand, the Notary Public who had an unusual physical problem like that of Queen Elizabeth, or so it was said. The violence, like an endless, shuddering earthquake, was frightening. Even dog, cat and bird were upon each other. A bevy of prostitutes came in by bus from a couple of big cities, rather good ones, not the oil-field type, but some pretty good ones from Houston and Dallas. The town was a boom town, like the old oil-strike days. But in this case oil was sex. The few hotels were packed and trailers came in. Tents were pitched, fast. A carnival diverted its rather unsuccessful tour of the Midwest and rushed down. Even the carnival people, though, didn't work much, they were immediately caught up in the frenzy—an ungodly sight (some said the few animals in the shabby sideshow—an old lion and lioness and a couple of tired boa constrictors went to it). The Siamese twins, an inferior pair—the better specimens were in big-time New York and Miami circuses, a small show has to take what it can pay for: top deformity acts get top money; the Frog Boy—my God, I can't go into it; but can I help it, what went on? That's what happened. And on slept the cause of it all, with his unyielding, his unshrinking, his risen "phallus". *Priapism*,

Ha! It was now seven days that he had held the world at bay with a loaded pistol.

But once it had reached its peak, this sweetness came over the place. After this first phase of wildness, the second began. Spent of its sort of bridal passion, its first fucking fury exhausted, the town moved into a curious kind of dignity. An idolatrous pride in Mr. de Persia pervaded. Reports that there were plans to steal him kept coming in, however. He had become very valuable, a treasure worth a lot. It was feared that he might be stolen like the precious saints' bodies were; and so the guard was doubled after it was decided not to remove the blessed body to the Church for safety. He now received the special care that is given to a statue of a hero, a monument in a park, a sainted figure. Once vulgarity and bestiality had expressed themselves, a new spirit set in: one of self-confidence, self-esteem, and vitality. And then *joy*. Why nobody had known the feeling of joy for years. There was, besides joy, gaiety, a feeling people hadn't known before. All this came from the wonderful figure in the glass tub, the beloved Mr. de Persia. He was the world's bridegroom, he was everybody's dream. The unconsummated bridegroom! The unsatisfied husband! The whole configuration of fundamental splendid man in the happy glass produced in the world around him a teased serenity, a slightly naughty glee, a sweet mischief. New life sprang from this happy figure and touched a community: Mr. de Persia, toucher and re-toucher! Also, and more important than anything else, people who had for a long time felt anger or guilt or unforgiveness had fucked it off and away, so that there was a spirit of reconciliation among the people. Out of the flesh had come a spiritual thing. How was it that what lay as pure sprawled-out and up-hard flesh could, in time, become pure spirit? Perplexion! Great mystery! And

what did it mean? a figure laid out like this, charged, un-is-
sued, without outcome? There were, moreover, certainly and
most obviously, magical powers in Mr. de Persia—people had
always known and seen that in him. And now he probably
was a medium for departed Spirits. You could stand in line
and take your turn to try to use him as a psychic medium—al-
lotted time two minutes, not much time for Spirits to get to
such an out-of-the-way place as Rose, Texas, and then, if
they did, not time for much contact and exchange; but not a
few people (one a famous Seer from California) got messages from the other world. When interviewed, she said some
of the messages were (amazingly terse) "Go North," "Get
lost," "Esther sucks"—an obvious confusion of interfering de-
monic and blessed spirits warring within the medium himself
—and so *like* him.

Yet where and who was the Charmer of all this? Obviously
a woman and she was under search, you can be sure. Why
would they want to punish the Charmer? For what? For this
gift to everybody? Why did they want to find her? Well, of
course, to unlock Mr. de Persia from his chains and bonds of
sleep. And, my God, to relieve him. He must be in pain. All
the physical aspects must be thought of, must be considered;
and now people were beginning to get sensible and practical
about what had overturned them and crazed them. Until they
discovered the Charmer, couldn't something else be done, like
give him a shot? Sort of sacrificial women were thought of—
and their number was legion—who would be willing as a
means of relieving or "changing" Mr. de Persia's condition—
that is, everything but the sleep part. But who knew, maybe
if they could get *that* down, like a sort of lever, it might raise
him up. Use it as a kind of crank, a gear to set the benumbed
man in motion! "Only one way to get rid of what's bothering
Mr. de Persia," the postmaster said. "And that's *not* a cold
shower." "We could haul him around and stud him off on the
towns," was another suggestion. Others said that they could
pimp him to widows, virgin brides who could then be pre-

pared for what was coming, unsatisfied wives. The list of possibilities was large.

The poor magician-in-spite-of-herself! What must she—for it was now assumed it could only be a woman—be feeling? Was she, disguised, among the thousands who came to view Mr. de Persia? Was she still in the town hiding out someplace? A hundred questions! She must be so embarrassed because of the stupid trick she pulled, or so afraid—a hundred feelings people imagined her to be feeling and suffering. Among all the other emotions flickering over the town was that of just a faint suspicion, a slight mistrust of odd-looking visitors or abnormally behaving local folks. Still, there was a lot of sentiment for the poor thing and great need of her. For God's sake wouldn't she come forward! Signs, ads, radio announcements, newspaper pleas, leaflets, church sermons—all asked only that the bewitcher of Mr. de Persia come forth and release him from the sleep he had been put into by a misused charm.

But then what *was* the charm? came the resounding question. How had it worked? Had Mr. de Persia been in a crucial phase of sexual excitement, *in or out,* when the spell was cast? Then *this* would not only be extraordinary but devilish, a real mean trick! A punishment? An act of vengeance?

These thoughts, then, cast a new color, another light, weird and uncanny and mysterious as the Charmer. She must be a bitch! A sorceress, a witch. A *castrater!* came the second piece of medical insight from the New York doctor, who had now enlisted the aid of a special and renowned Psychologist from Zürich, Switzerland, to act as a consultant. (I needn't tell you that Mr. de Persia's notoriety had now reached Europe, and photographs—sometimes close-ups—of him lying in the glass cask had appeared in *Paris Match, Die Welt,* and an Italian magazine which reproduced the photograph in color.) Enough sheep had been cut for local people to know the meaning of the Swiss Psychologist's word—it had a local practical purpose and a practical meaning; but used in this way, it was not clear to many. Several people told him to go screw himself which, under the circumstances, seemed a helpful, even humane suggestion to Mr. de Persia, could he hear it.

Which led to the longing wish that if only Mr. de Persia could help himself. The irony was that Mr. de Persia himself was the only one around who could get this man out of his plight, knowing the solution to the charm which imprisoned him, yet here *he* was the very victim! For Mr. de Persia had solved many a local puzzle, broken a lot of cases of mystery, opened impossible locks (the bigger the lock the more sensitive the instrument you use against it, he said. It was with the big brute heavy things that he used his light hand. His heavy hand held it but his light hand did the delicate work.) He had never, of course, raised up anybody under a spell like himself, but it was generally believed that he could do so were it necessary. Now here the raiser lay himself unraised—except in the most personal way. But he had divined several things that had bestowed reputation and authority upon himself. He knew where to look for lost objects—he found eyeglasses, lost purses, rings, poll-taxes, driver's licenses; even stolen things came to light under his discovering genius; he located cars, letters, jewels; and once in a while he had been able to lay hands on the whereabouts of a thief, a missing person, someone hiding out, and other mysteries. Mechanically gifted, a genius at creating complicated constructions, he had constructed a delicate, efficient world of contrivances composed of levers and purchases, slings, tension springs, gears, trestles, trapezes, pulleys and braces for the crippled to survive in, for the limbless (arms, hands, legs, feet) to travel with (drive, walk, even dance). Therefore the afflicted loved him. He was, then, a healer—a creator, really—for he had made new people; they sort of rose from the dead, because where they had been halt before, now they could walk, even though mechanically, like crabs, like robots or puppets; and where they'd be flat on their backs paralyzed, he raised them up on trapezes and slings with ropes and pulleys. Mr. de Persia set a whole still world of people into motion, as though he had brought them to life. Naturally, the afflicted and deformed loved him and considered him their savior.

He made a deaf lady hear, though later, God knows, she wished she hadn't from some of the things she heard. But he made her a horn for people to speak in, yelling a little, and she could hear. The horn was made of shining brass and on it the creator had inscribed O World O Life O Time. A very ugly woman named Theresa was blind in one eye because of a dropped eyelid—it had fallen like a broken shutter and darkened that side of her. What Mr. de Persia did was to draw the eyelid up with an invisible thread and tie it around the lady's ear and she rejoiced. "I got so tired of looking at the inside of my eyelid," she said. "Now I can see something else, for a change. And when there's something I don't want to see, why I just pull the invisible string and down goes the curtain on something I can't stand to see. Mr. de Persia gave me sight of things, though, where I had only half before."

He was a master inventor, no doubt about it. With wires and strings he could raise up into a lifelike position a dead bird so quick on the wing that a hunter would have shot at it. Once he devised a grabbing contraption that worked like a hand turned by an elbow to reach down, clutch and pull up a boy who had fallen in a dry well. He had performed, with a gadget that burrowed and kicked out dirt like a possum, excavations under fallen masses; had snagged thrashing people drowning in the river, rescued people from flames in hotel fires with instant ladders that shot out, jointed, from an object no bigger than a stepladder; and, in general, he had done heroic, lifesaving acts at the mill and other places. He was a saint! A hero! A mastermind! Now he was of no help to anybody, including himself. He just lay radiant, as if he were in a glossy cake of gelatin, man-in-aspic, something exquisite and gourmet, his countenance rosy with strange health and his body warm and blooming. He was obviously thriving in very deep life.

Once their energy was recovered a little, the people of the

town began to do more constructive planning. First, they moved Mr. de Persia in his tub from his overcrowded repair shop. He needed a large and open place. They had to take off part of the roof, and since the big man in glass could absolutely not be lifted, a crane was brought over from Conroe. People along the way who saw it traveling like some dinosaur with police cars howling around it, told each other that that was the crane from Conroe going to lift up Mr. de Persia in the glass tub. A tremendous procession gathered and followed.

The crowd that had assembled to witness the transfer of Mr. de Persia in the glass tub was in need of police control, for there were thousands. And there, in the sunlit air rose the gleaming burden of the crane, which seemed to do its work with slow and measured majesty. Caught for a moment in the direct rays of the sun, it shot out a blinding flash of light that struck the crowd like lightning and the thousands wove and shuddered under the dazzling glance and it was mysterious and pentacostal and many fell or were cast to the ground like Paul in his blind seizure. In a second it was over; and down, shining as lucently and silvery as if it were a cake of ice in tongs, the tub of glass lightly lowered onto a pipeline truck and was carried as carefully as an egg to Rose Field on the edge of town, the site of Chautauquas, Revivals, and Carnivals, since this was the largest open space with shelter—the covered bandstand—that could be found.

The tub rested on the bandstand stage under the great shell of the open-air platform, raised high—just above reach—so that people could not molest Mr. de Persia. To see him up there above, through the glass, he was something more than a man. He was of nature, something in a jar—fruit, preserve; something aquarian—a purplish fish. At times the glass became like flesh, pale and smooth-looking, soft as skin. Other times it was incandescent in the hot noon sun, livid with white heat, so that Mr. de Persia's body seemed incendiary in white flame, transfigured. But at night the ice was all frozen azure and the figure lay now cold and hard and remote, and seemed smaller. And at darkest night, the glass was opaque and almost black. Then, in the light of dawn, people came quietly before sunrise to see, in awe, the glass become a piece of cold white water. And then, when the sunrise struck it like a flaming sword and marked an orange cross over it, people fell to their knees and wept and confessed.

But at all times, Mr. de Persia remained mysteriously fresh and unruffled, his suit fresh, his body sweet and untouched by time. His amazing freshness and purity, the miracle of his self-refreshment, of his being unravaged by the passage of time, untouched by material changes and physical needs, save his unappeasable and inexhaustible power, curved like a horn across his thigh, peaking like a large bonnet his purple trousers, made him seem immortal, beyond rust and moth. He dwelt in many mansions, in his tub. Yet how very mortal he was as he went on breathing gruffly, like a great male, and lifting from himself, buoyant and graceful as a bending reed and solid as a sausage, his throbbing flesh.

The wall behind this now apostolic figure was garlanded with strings of bright flowers and streamers of colored paper, branches of pine trees, and it was a real bower. Rose Field became a wide plaza where the crowds could mill or stand.

Now that Mr. de Persia had space around him, hundreds and hundreds more began to come to him in search of his widely publicized powers. Now, not only the curious, the lecherous and the adoring came, but also the afflicted. People came shouting because they were deaf and could not hear themselves talk, staggering on crutches because they were crippled, and led by others because they were blind. Others were brought on cots and there were even humpbacks, hare-lips, grossly fat people, and an assortment of your usual run of deformities including, it was said, a morphodite from Grape-land. It is not known whether there were any restorations or healings, but it was reported that an old woman, blind since birth, got something of a glimpse, just for a few moments, of her sister who had taken care of her all these years. "I saw Elva, I saw Elva!" she cried, and danced for joy until she fell down. When they picked her up, she was blind again. But she gave testimonials, although it had not been Elva at all that she had seen, because Elva had asked an old man to watch after her sister for a minute while she went to buy some chewing gum.

So now Mr. de Persia had a reputation like a god: he held power over growth and decay, over a kind of birth and a kind of death, over "failing energies" as a Boston newspaper had put it. Mr. de Persia, virtuoso inventor, elite fixer, visionary artificer, restorer, *magnifico, fantastico* as the Italian press named him, came to stand for art, life-in-death, sex, and human folly. He who had wanted to repair and mend the broken chain of life as if he were to solder broken metal links in his shop, lay now in chaste lust, raunchy abstinence, hot purity, somewhat divine.

It was on the twenty-eighth day of his "lubricious sleep" (a phrase applied to Mr. de Persia by a London newspaper report) that Mr. de Persia's body was found missing at dawn.

3
The Pursuit of
Mr. de Persia

The guards had fallen asleep. Their excuses were muddled. Had they heard a sound? How long were they asleep? Had they felt drugged or some spell come over them? They just couldn't say. They were stupefied and furious with the thief. Had somebody put a potion in their coffee? Who brought the coffee? Talented Sylvan Morgan, whose father owned Morgan's store, and was planning any day to leave town and go to a City and get in a show. Well, find Sylvan Morgan! But apparently he had suddenly decided to leave earlier than he'd planned, for he was nowhere to be found. A real *suspect!* the papers declared. 1814231

Had the guards waked up with erections? Yes, but they always woke up that way. Had the guards, who by now had turned upon each other in rage and guilt at having lost the treasure, not been protected, the town would've stoned them to death, or seized them and hanged them. There were threats of castrating them. The guards were locked up in jail, and themselves put under guard—the very guards of Mr. de Persia were guarded! Even then, one of them, a young, excitable and fanatic worshiper of Mr. de Persia, committed suicide in the night.

Now there was an uproar, not only in the town but nationwide, and there were repercussions worldwide. So many

questions swarmed: had the sorceress come again and spelled
Mr. de Persia away? Had his body been stolen by bigtime
thieves, Mafia, gangsters, people with plans to make a lot of
money off him, or had Mr. de Persia simply waked up and
slipped away? The glass tub had lost its light, and, beautiful
an object as it was in itself, fell desolate and lifeless-looking
without its fantastic occupant. The town fell into grief and
bitter rage—it was torn apart.

What stirred the magic sleeper? What disturbed this figure
of splendor? What broke his enchanted dream and started
Mr. de Persia up into life again? Where had he gone? A light
went out in the world and in the glass tub. It now stood
there drab as a woodbox in the forlorn field. A glory was
gone from this old earth.

There was a fast and militant organization of forces. A
squadron of searchers was formed to ferret about on foot,
searching every corner of the town. These were meticulous
and cunning old people who knew how to comb and pick
through. The kind that—God deliver you from them if you're
a sales clerk—leave nothing unturned. Such stealthy old ones
pick up the sense of a dark scene like a rat. A furious posse of
chasers, young buck studs, was put on horseback, one mass of
rearing, stomping, shouting man and animal, and they thundered out of town towards where nobody was sure; and a
mixed band of young and old who knew the mysterious
Thicket went into its wilderness and began flushing out with
dog and stick, blazing trails, and unlocking locked brambles
with hatchet and knife. They saw the old bearded hermit—
the Gregarious Recluse—always seen by hunters and adven-
turers. Some still insisted that he had horns. To be such a her-

mit who had made the decision to remove himself from social intercourse, he always came very easily into the hands of strangers, like an easy woman or a wagging puppy and would talk your right arm off if you let him, sentimental old soft lovable slob.

A pair of people, an ungodly duo made up of a fake priest and a transvestite, were spied on the highway in a pickup truck and seized near the Louisiana line, transporting and smuggling a dummy of Mr. de Persia, so lifelike that it was astonishing, out of the State. "We were just having some fun," the transvestite, only in half-drag (he wore denim pants and cowboy boots but was in heavy stage eye and face makeup and filled out a flimsy blouse) declared. "We were just moving a little magic along Highway 6A through this ugliness of billboards and Pig Stands where the barbecue is all fat," said the young transvestite. "To bring people some magic."

"And a little Jesus Christ for their hearts," chimed the priest.

"Come on," the policeman said firmly. "Follow us. You're under arrest although we don't know what for yet."

"The Mann Act?" asked the young man in his half-drag. "Ha!"

"Buddy you wouldn't know a man from a towsack."

"Don't kid yourself. But in this instance you're no use in helping me recognize one," lisped the young transvestite. The cop looked closely at his giant clashing eyelashes, the gleaming wet-orange lips, the sooty mascara, and chuckled out like an oath, "Cheesuh Christ!"

"What's your problem *now?*" asked the drag queen.

"Because I recognize you as Sylvan Morgan!" gasped the cop. "I oughta whip your ass!"

Then Sylvan Morgan suddenly jumped into the pickup and lifted the stuffed replica of Mr. de Persia, unzipped his trousers and released an immense organ of rubber that bobbed and waved thickly above huge hanging testicles and did obscene acts with it, screaming with delight, while the fake

priest held his raised eyes toward heaven and clasped his
hands, from which a long rosary hung. This was their Act, a
piece of early pornography in Texas. The highway patrolman
did the only thing he knew to do and that was to confiscate
the straw-and-rag Mr. de Persia. What a superb joy Sylvan
Morgan had done; he was talented, no question. The policeman seized the dummy and in the struggle clasped it to him
in a sort of dancing position. "Oooo!" shrieked Sylvan Morgan,
"may I cut in, ha!" and the two began a tug of war on Mr. de
Persia's replica. The poor phony priest was running up and
down and calling out to the Saints. Whoever was crossing the
Louisiana state line that day you'd have thought would have
kept going, seeing such a crazy sight in the back of a pickup
truck. But no, of course highway travelers stopped, and seeing what it was, joined in the tug of war. That was how the
dummy Mr. de Persia was torn to pieces (cotton wads, newspapers, excelsior straw) and scattered by the wind over the
Louisiana line. Some found pieces and gobs of him floating on
the Gulf at Biloxi, even; and the fake Mr. de Persia was
picked out of trees as far as the Valley. The two thieves fled,
in the commotion, and were lost; who cared. The rubber phallus—which of course everyone was after—people have no conscience—was seen floating on the river through several towns,
and there was seining and there were nets and devices of all
kinds to try to capture the floating organ of Mr. de Persia,
said, now, to have supernatural and magical powers. But it
reached the river's mouth at Boca Chica, was detected among
garbage and sewage, swirling into the foul Gulf at Browns-
ville, where a lighthouse keeper reported to Associated Press
that he saw a seagull carrying it away toward Mexico—people
in Mexico *did* see a UFO, but who knew?—a tanker going
from Houston to Balboa, Panama, telegraphed sighting it
among a company of dolphins who were having themselves a
time with it; and finally there was silence, it was seen no
more. Mr. de Persia's rubber private had disappeared forever.

The town was left with the empty tub of glass. Though it

couldn't be moved, of course, and was therefore not in danger of being stolen, the round-the-clock guard continued. A famous lawyer and a famous detective came to try to solve the case. More people poured in. So many journalists and press reporters were there that they had to set up a special tent for their headquarters. There was a blue balloon always over the town, buzzardlike, radio-broadcasting, photographing, advertising. It rose from and settled in a pasture behind Rose Field. It flew out a streamer that unrolled like a paper whistle and it advertised various commodities—"Eat," "Drink," "Chew," "Buy." The balloon also took photographs of Mr. de Persia for publicity releases to newspapers all over everywhere and for local sale. Thousands of photos were sold. A framed picture of Mr. de Persia in his glass tub was on the walls of most houses and in stores and offices along with the Pope, the President, and Jesus Christ, in many instances. Poor Mr. de Persia! He was truly on everybody's lips and in their prayers, that no harm would come to him, asleep or awake, wherever he was.

Suddenly he was seen walking in the river bottom, by some early morning fishermen. Two men swore they saw him walking in the dawn river-fog along the riverbank. Instead of calling to him, they fled. At the Jake & Lou Diner (Jake was a woman) by the crossroads, the fishermen called in to the newspaper. A search was rushed out and put to foot in that area but nothing was found. A bullhorn was even used, calling, "Mr. de Persia! Mr. de Persia!" It resounded through the river woods, and sounded very eerie. Birds flew up and there were crashing sounds of animals leaping away.

One fear was that the sleeper might be walking around in the trance that had laid him low. This thought was horrifying to some, as though he might have been a human monster, stalking at night. Naturally there were more and more visions of the walking sleeper—at windows in the night, in orchards by moonlight, in trees out by the lake. One person saw him sitting in the barber chair at the hotel barbershop around two in the morning. If he was mobile now—"ambulatory" was the word they were using—was he still *in erectus?*—a phrase used by some newspaper writers or *Time* or somebody. (We were all getting quite an education and our vocabulary was enlarged and enriched. Mr. de Persia's condition was affording us fast, free experience. We would never be the same; we knew too much now. In this way the town was corrupted by Mr. de Persia. Our innocence had departed. In this way Mr. de Persia had raped the virgin town of Rose, Texas. We had eaten his apple; as they said in the cities, we'd been *fucked.* Both ways.) My God, many a bedroom occupant thought it had a visitor in the night. Local daydreams were rampant, now that Mr. de Persia might be accessible.

In the absence of the very man himself, the ghost of Mr. de Persia took over the town. His absence possessed the town as powerfully as his presence had. There was no escaping him. No wonder people said he was a magic man and gave him supernatural powers and qualities of a wonder person. There were sudden sights of him, and at the oddest times, and in the most unlikely places. Sometimes he was naked, a huge god-like figure resembling a statue in a museum, with his great stob of a phallus stabbed into him, and his testicles like a fat apple between his thighs. Once he was carring young Jesus on his back. Another time he was strolling with a woman, and then somebody again had that same sight of him, and then one more. Who was this woman? All those who had seen her described her the same. She was tall and dark-headed and veiled! How? Hooded, almost, with lots of white veils over her dark hair and face, burning eyes, glowing behind the silken folds. But the woman remained a mystery and nothing ever materialized. False alarm! Blind alley!

4

The Taking Up
of Mr. de Persia

The truth of it is, the robbers of the glass tub, thieves of Mr. de Persia's precious person (it was now worth a ransom of thousands), held him captive in the blue balloon.

The thieves were two young men and a young woman. They were all no more than twenty years old, or so they appeared through binoculars. The three had whisked (if you could *whisk* a great body like Mr. de Persia) the body away like true professionals, and apparently as lightly as angels carry the departed. The town had thought they were the photographers—who in truth lay gagged in a nearby gully. As though they were rescuing someone from water, they hovered, dropped a sling with two men clinging to it like insects. In a flashing moment, the two men deftly slipped the sling under Mr. de Persia's arms and up rose all three as lightly as aerialists, and the balloon floated away.

Who saw Mr. de Persia's ascension over East Texas that misty morning? The three guards certainly did not. They were off in the wings with three teen-age girls who came at the same time every dark morning before dawn. Since they thought they were being photographed when they saw the balloon, they all cringed together in a mass, burrowing and hiding their faces under one another like animals keeping warm, and so saw nothing. But the thieves in the balloon had not only taken Mr. de Persia, they had taken photographs which later proved that the guards had not, as they had said, fallen asleep, and which were sold under the counter for a price.

What was that falling out of the sky one morning? Fingers pointed to something high, high up, flashing like a silver leaf, something turning in the light. Then it was lost in the darkness behind cloud. Something was falling, then rising again. There was a feeling of terror over the town, it was like the end of the world. People in backtowns, hidden bayou towns and in the swamp who suddenly saw a shape in the sky, fell to the ground on their knees or ran into their root cellars, shaking and praying, believing it to be the end of the world. All day the whole world of Thicket towns was haunted and scared to death.

When it dropped low over the town of Rose, people saw the blue balloon trailing its streamer. It read: WE'VE GOT HIM. "He's in the blue balloon!" the cry went up from the town. Now the town was shocked and dumbfounded and everyone felt helpless. How in God's name could you capture a man held prisoner in a floating balloon? Well, the balloon would have to come down. Its floating duration was pretty short. If it came down low enough, cowboys said they could lasso it.

But the blue balloon was riding the wind in a Gulf current that kept it amazingly aloft. It hunted for wind and got caught in an elevator of rising air and lifted upward, wallowing lazily in the draughts, until it settled softly on a miraculous cushion of wind, springy and holding it aloft like waterwings, and there it was sustained, sliding sideways over East Texas without a care in the world. The girl in the basket was playing an Irish harp and the music of the harp fell down sweetly over the countryside and some thought they were in their eternity, such celestial and angelic harmonies tinkled

down in glassy cascades, chining and fluting and thrumming.
How odd the world had become, like a dream or a vision or
some kind of madness!

What people below didn't know was that the girl in the
balloon had pulled up her skirt and straddled Mr. de Persia.
Her motive was not strictly self-satisfaction—so many had
tried to get at Mr. de Persia who seemed to be offering a
helluva good time to somebody—it was a martyr's desire to
perpetuate the great fabricator that sat her astride Mr. de
Persia, riding him in midair on a June afternoon in a blue balloon.

But was it a fountain that never went dry? The girl, whose
name was Selina Rosheen, was a mysterious and lustful
beauty who had come into town—because of the de Persia notoriety—from where no one knew—she was probably a Gypsy,
a Mexican, someone of strange and exotic race—who knew?
Although Selina Rosheen was filled brimming with the rich
and magic elixir of Mr. de Persia, there was no sign on the
great man of his loss. Upraised he remained, the indefatigable
sleeper. Selina Rosheen swore that Mr. de Persia moved a little. "He could make an army!" Selina exclaimed. "But I've got
what I wanted out of him. I can tell."

Two and a half years later a baby boy, somewhat over a
year old, it was guessed, was found in a hollow log at the edge
of the Thicket near Camden. A sawmill man named Leander
Suggins, going to work to cut trees in the Thicket, heard the
cries and found the child. It was in good health, except for a
wound on the inside of its thigh near its sex that looked like
the bite of a serpent and was the shape of a harp.

Leander's wife, Nesta, part Indian and one-third Mexican,
the rest Scotch-Irish, she told everybody, found it hard to believe Leander's story. "Don't come home to tell me you found

a baby in a log. You been straddling that log. Knowing you, I wouldn't doubt it, you'd straddle anything that's got a hole in it." Naturally there were lots of stories among the men about Leander and the hollow log, Leander and the knothole, etc.

But the sight of Leander Suggins and the baby walking down the road to the Orphans Home with the baby bottle of milk in his hip pocket was sweet. For some moments he wanted to keep the baby because it felt so warm and alive in his arms and gave him a feeling he'd never had before that he couldn't name. But it was out of the question because Nesta wanted to work all day in her Hair Salon which she had developed through hard work and a natural talent and had no interest in a baby. That was why he two-timed her sometimes that made him suffer so much afterwards—because she wouldn't let him have it as often as he needed it, which was just about every noon and night, because she didn't want to get pregnant.

"You little bugger," Leander said to the baby as he walked down the road to the Orphans Home up at Longview. After he left the baby on the road he kept looking back at the gray lonesome-looking house that was the Orphans Home until it went out of sight around a bend; and when he got home he went and got drunk and it was after some time then that one of his drinking buddies discovered the baby bottle still in his hip pocket. Leander defended the bottle with such a rage that he just about started a drunken fistfight and nobody succeeded in getting the baby bottle away from him. Walking home drunk, he held the bottle close to him and felt such an old sorrow that he cried in low sobs—why, he couldn't fully understand, but it had a lot to do with his suddenly realizing that he was tired and lonesome in this life of hard day-labor work and of being poor and it also had to do with the baby and his feeling for it, he knew. He stumbled home and in his drunkenness hid the baby bottle under his pillow where he found, in the morning, that it had squirted out milk through its nipple as he turned his heavy head on it. When he got up he hid the bottle in his work clothes and later, in the Thicket at lunchtime, he went off and buried the baby bottle under a young white hawthorn, as if the baby he found in the log had died.

Then it was Ace Adair one day, coming up the same road after the little orphan Addis to adopt him for Jewel. The Methodist Church in Rose, under the auspices of the Ladies' Missionary Society and with the help of Reverend Bill Jack Pugh—he was called Brother Bill Jack—had helped Jewel with her application and all the red tape you had to do to adopt a baby.

But more about Ace Adair and Jewel and Addis later, and back, now, to Mr. de Persia.

5

The Captivity
of Mr. de Persia

The three robbers and Mr. de Persia, now in his aerial sleep, drifted over town in the misty dawn. They had carefully and lovingly put their precious cargo on a soft mattress covered with a silken sheet; and under his head was a silken pillow of pale blue. Mr. de Persia lay in the straw basket like a celestial emperor of the upper air, wafting over the world. His miraculous freshness and purity still kept him sweet, clean and unruffled. How warm he was to the touch of the three robbers! They caressed and embraced and fondled the wonderful cargo of the balloon, the precious prisoner of sleep and air.

They drifted aloft in a kind of dream, over the dozing countryside of East Texas, in the soft light, in the silken basket. The basket was made of open wickerwork and the sweet air blew softly through it. The purple figure of Mr. de Persia flashing in the light of sun or moon—or later by floodlight and searchlight—could be seen from below. And the balloon rode on in the sweet heights, slipping over the silken currents of a wide sweet river of air, a gentle velvet surf, on the velvet crest of long gentle swells of warm sensual wind. Sometimes it was bathed by gray cool fogs and by the chill mists of aromatic clouds as if they were spiced. Its passengers knew paradise days, harp-charmed, and their nights were under silver stars that rose and dipped, swayed and sagged, and a yellow quarter-moon that rocked like a cradle and hung low enough for an anchor.

The town was afoot and aghast. It stood in fields, on roads, on rooftops, tops of buildings, looking up. Oil derricks were covered with people hanging from them. Lighthouses beaconed at night on the Gulf and ships on the Gulf kept watch and flashed their lights. But Mr. de Persia was out of reach. Over a tranquil countryside already changing and fading away and dying, something he could not redeem or restore like the photographs—the little town, the green woods, the sweet rivers, fresh-growing farmlands, meadows and pastures, the far green Gulf, the twisting Thicket—Mr. de Persia, the restorer, the repairman, maker and saver, gently rocked and drifted.

Plans to recover Mr. de Persia were numerous. How could you chase a balloon? What with all the Texas Rangers in Texas, all the Militiamen in the State, no opposition on the ground was any good. And if you shot the balloon down that would be the end of Mr. de Persia.

The town, even the world, waited. In a violent thunderstorm there were fears for the balloon, but it came through. Sometimes it would soar so high that it was lost to view. On one cloudy afternoon it was hidden and the town was uneasy; then the balloon broke through a clearing, and there were hurrahs and all was well. Cheers went up.

But like a hound sniffing and trailing them, came an airplane with a star on it, sent up by the Army. The chase began. It was such a soft midsummer day with big clouds rolling as slow as the balloon. Thousands watched the game in the air. Soon the harp fell, dangling from a blue parachute. They were lightening the blue balloon to make it rise higher. The harp softly spun and swung under its parachute as it came down. And up rose the blue balloon. Up, also, rose the little plane, buzzing like an insect, circling and dipping and diving. It made noisy passes at the balloon. But what could it do? The balloon sailed on.

About 5 P.M. one afternoon, eight days after the balloon had robbed the glass tub of Mr. de Persia, out of the balloon dropped Mr. de Persia, pale purple in the waning light, dangling from a white parachute. Mr. de Persia was falling to earth. Down he floated, sliding suddenly to one side, drifting to the other, then seeming to hang still in the air. And then Mr. de Persia sank into the Thicket. The balloon drifted on eastward, toward the Gulf, and some say they saw it collapse like a tent and fall into the Gulf. Others saw three parachutes lowering over Mexico. But nothing of the three robbers and the balloon was ever heard again.

A search began, reached a frenzied peak, and then subsided. No one found Mr. de Persia. Nothing, no trace was known of his fate whether he was devoured by wild beasts of the Thicket, whether he was taken by Gypsies or runaway Coushata Indians, or by hiding escaped convicts, or whether he lived on as a sleeping prisoner deep in the thick, shady wilderness, a part of wild nature, sleeping on through the decades. The search for him went on. He became a legend. It was concluded that the sleeping spell which glorified him had also eliminated him, that his triumph was his loss. His banishment might therefore be considered tragic were it not for the fact that Mr. de Persia was not considered to be gone forever but would one day return. He was waited for, vivaciously expected. Mr. de Persia joined that ancient body of legend that had to do with comings back, with expectations, returns.

But he was nevertheless still searched for. From time to time a man would rise up in a kind of rabid possession and go alone into the wilderness in a fanatic avowal to find him; or men would organize an expedition and enter the Thicket, determined to find the now almost sacred body, living or dead,

of Mr. de Persia. They would tell tales of ghosts and haunted
figures in the Thicket when they came out, unsuccessful. The
old hermit was captured by searchers for the hundredth time:
poor thing, he slipped into captor's hands as easily as a dying
fish in the water, he could never find any of the peace that he
sought among or away from humanity. He was thoroughly in-
terrogated. But he knew nothing of Mr. de Persia, and
thought his questioners crazy to be asking such questions. It
must have made him relieved to know he was out of the society of men. The derelict Coushata brave, outcast by his
tribe or self-exiled, in his poor insane way, indicated nothing.
He had, he informed them, discovered a magic berry which
would cause visions of God.

The hidden years of Mr. de Persia in the wilds remained a
mystery. What visions he saw, what sufferings, what lonesomeness ached him, there in the wilderness Thicket among
the wild creatures, the ancient, motherly trees, the green life,
will never be known, only conjectured, by history. What had
he to do with Rose? His legacy was unusual and few know it.
What he left behind—besides the notorious glass tub—a mas-
terpiece—were frail designs and graceful figures. He had
touched Rose like a kind of weather—frost, crystal, ice; and
like the seasons he left fruit, nuts, leaves, blossoms. And he
fashioned a dashing, energetic, gleeful and fiendishly indus-
trious red Devil for a teen-age oilfire-fighter's back. Some say,
therefore, that he put the Devil on Wylie Prescott's back; considered Mr. de Persia, therefore, a handman of the Devil,
Devil's tool. But that's just another version of the legendary
Mr. de Persia—never was another'n like him. And it's probably what was then just a funny kind of a gadget made of
brass that turned out to be an indispensable oilwell thinga-
mabob—worth millions.

How old was he at the time of his disappearance? He was
about fifty at the time (Jewel Adair would be, I guess, about
forty by now . . . let's see—if she was something like twenty
when Addis was adopted, and Ace about twenty-one, and

Addis vanished when he was fifteen, she'd be *thirty-three* or so at that time, so I'm wrong about her being forty. She was in her early thirties.) But guess Mr. de Persia was crowding fifty, and a strong-armed, virile man; strong-backed, too, 'twas said; he was a bachelor and had, 'twas known and reported, been into every willing woman in this town and the next, and attempted a few unwilling ones . . . with success, I'm told. One was Jane Allen Clumson, said she kept saying no, no, no, don't, you don't have my permission; but he went right on, anyway, and so did Jane Allen Clumson—two more times, I know for a fact because Jane Allen Clumson told me.

In a history of early Rose, wonder what Mr. de Persia would be chronicled as? A sorcerer? Wizard? A genius? A beloved cheat? He did become the sort of spirit of Rose for a period in its early development; and once when it snowed, a sculpture of a sleeping figure commemorating him stood for a while in a local field until it melted.

But one man goes down, another rises in life—which is, after all, if you think about it, an arrangement of risings and fallings, ends and beginnings, deaths and resurrections.

6
Addis
Adair

Now Addis Adair was an adopted boy, adopted by Jewel and Ace Adair when he was a little thing, no more than three years old. The town spoke of him as one who had a virgin mother and was a son without a father (and spoke of his adopted father, Ace, as a man who had a virgin wife). And a superstition developed about Addis Adair, as happens in towns, that said he was of miraculous birth since it was obvious to all and known by a few who passed it on, that his mother was a virgin; said he had special powers, said he was a wonder child, a holy child; some said he was Satan disguised and should be kept locked up at home.

His adopted father, Ace Adair, was a dark handsome man, died from falling (*some* said), drunk, under the wheels of a switch engine in the roundhouse at the edge of town (long since gone, of course, though the shell of it is back yonder, shattered glass roof fallen, wild blooming vines gnarled as big as trees, and a living garden of snakes, 'tis said, a Satanish place). At any rate, the talk was that Jewel Adair would never let her husband Ace touch her but one time (one *half* time, really) and so he drank himself to death, in miserable chastity, an ungiven sensual saint, a true saint was Ace Adair. But more of that later and now back to Addis Adair.

Addis Adair grew up under the shadow of his false mother.

He scarcely got to know his unreal father (that is, not his real one). For poor Ace Adair, after a few years of misery, went down, as I have told you, in the sunken locomotive. Addis was about five at this time. This left Jewel to raise him up without the interference of Ace and she never let him out of her sight; sat over him as he slept at night and adored him, staring on him for hours without flinching; she was seen through the window doing this by lamplight, studying the child, Addis Adair, as if in a trance.

And so Addis grew up to something like fourteen, a strange boy, beautiful and dark (what was his blood, the town asked, was it Jewish, was it part Nigra, was it Cajun, what was it that give him his foreign look?). And naturally the day came when Addis suddenly rose up and said to Jewel: Woman what do you have to do with me? (poor Jewel) and went away. Jewel became quite crazy. No one could come near her; she'd go after them like a setting hen; she sulked alone back in the old Adair house (Ace's grandparents had built it and lived and died there). Because you see Wylie Prescott's uncle was Ace Adair and his aunt was Jewel. Wylie's mother was Lucy Adair, Ace's sister who married a traveling drummer named Prescott and kept on traveling until he "wore out," kinfolks said, on the road, dying of a heart attack near Memphis in one year. Later Lucy Adair died. And Ace. And Jewel. Leaving Wylie Prescott there, in Rose, Texas, and Addis Adair's whereabouts unknown.

But back to where I was. Addis Adair vanished from the earth, apparently. In her trance, in Jewel's madness, he came to seem only a memory. She hid away, dreaming of the former times, and Rose, Texas let her alone. She talked out all night, sitting at a darkened window, waiting. She talked half to Mr. de Persia, half to Addis Adair. She implored them both; she sang out to them both. But Addis Adair was the burden of her deluded night-calling.

But Mr. de Persia oh you know what I would like to really have you bring me back; that's a boy, came here to me as just

*a little biddy thing and grew up on this place quiet as
though the Devil'd taken his tongue. Was not my own son yet
was all I had. Addis! Where'd he go, same place as you, some
land of vanishment; are you two together, maybe? If you
come back will he come back? Will I look out and see the two
of you coming back to me? What happened to 'im, why'd he
leave me; why'd he go? Find him! You was always good at
lost and found. You've found some things that were lost before—the opal ring that Lucius Seager's wife lost on the picnic;
you found that; you went into a kind of a trance and knitted
your brow so tight it joined your eyebrows together; and then
you murmured, I remember, "on a hand that has four fingers
rests an opal." Which meant that the only person in town
with four fingers—you know who, that lost her little finger in
the sewing machine—and there the opal was. You also named
the location, sitting up all night long in your meditation while
half the town waited and held quiet, too, oh my God, of the
poor drowned boy (is he drowned, oh Jesus mine is he lying
on the bottom of the water?): they dragged and found him.
Bring back Addis!*

But Addis did not come back. Nor Mr. de Persia. Or did
he? Did he hear Jewel's plaint and answer her call, knocking
at her window in the night, whispering Jewel! Jewel! I'm
here . . . ? Because one time after quite some time passed,
a flame was seen licking out of the chimney like a wicked
tongue out of the Adair house around midnight, and when the
firemen got there and put out a shingle fire caused by wood
sparks, they reported seeing a woman so unlike Jewel Adair
that they thought she was a visitor. "Where's Jewel Adair?"
the firemen asked. "You're looking at her," said the exciting-
looking woman. What the firemen said they saw was a luxu-
rious woman with flowing black hair and full white breasts.
Yet people took this as a joke on Jewel, a fireman's folly. Until another thing happened. Jewel Adair appeared again. She
was seen on her roof fixing a loose brick on the chimney.
She took her time. People came to look at her and they

watched her silently. She faced them head-on as she did her work and she was beautiful to see. Was this an announcement? She seemed ready for something. Was her appearance on her roof, taking her time and ease under the gaze of the townspeople, was this a proclamation of her return to the world? Was she joining the human race?

What had so changed Jewel Adair, who had risen like a Venus out of the old Jewel, a lightless woman who had driven her husband to die in drunken chastity and fouled desire in the iron tomb of a switch engine? Could a person become such an entirely different person, a new person? Jewel did. What did it?

The town now held her like a prize, its treasure. A rich man came from Oklahoma City to try to woo her to him, offering his crude oil fortune. The Town Council offered to redo—paint and repair—her house. Such a beautiful creature should inhabit a beautiful place, 'twas said. Boys came at night and crept around the house to see if they could glimpse her. Peeping Toms sprang up in the meadows and out of the woods around her house like jack-in-the-boxes. But nobody would molest Jewel because she was too grand and untouchable. She was not a hussy or a cheap woman. They looked upon her as a reserved queen in a castle.

But had she been a fireman's mirage, a drunk's ghost, a shadow made by the flame? Who knew?

Anyway, no matter what, after sinking into deep recollection and yearning for the lost days of Rose, she sprang up from the brooding depths of herself and changed, miraculously, her attitude. How, you wonder? Through Christian Science? through body control? beauty treatments? some potion? some magic? Through the actual coming of Mr. de Persia? And for what, you wonder? For destiny, or fate, or chance, or for her own judgment day, to do with her what they would? Well, Jewel's destiny was scheming something and her body was following it. In its solitude, what was her body brooding as she was enripening herself, her own sex in-

seminating itself? What was enriching within Jewel Adair,
Jewel so mysteriously enjuiced? In her lavish incarnation,
what had been on the verge of a harpy, a harridan, a crone,
an austere and devout and solemn, dried-up woman drab as
a Puritan and glum as a Penitente, had now become ripe
flesh with coal-black hair so luxuriant that she combed and
brushed it twice a day—in both places—and rising breasts
strutted with hormones and pale with the hunger to be
handled. What worked magic on Jewel Adair? Who cast this
spell over her to make her like a goddess? What enchanter?
Some said, again, that it was the old spellbound Mr. de Persia
at her, coming out of the Thicket at night to Jewel, called by
her through her long, all-night speeches and summonses which
were like mating calls bringing some wild gamey thing out of
the wilderness. And that whatever spell had been put on him
had now been passed on to her by him. That it was the old
powerhouse himself that changed Jewel, the old wizard restorer Mr. de Persia. But no one ever saw him, nor knew—it
was just talk and superstition, *probably.*

Or was it that, like wine or bulb or fruit, she had enriched
herself out of her own vitality, out of her own sap and juice
in the cellar or on the shelf of her deep self in the dark, waiting for Addis Adair to come back? Had her long solitude
ripened and plumped and enraptured her, waiting for Addis
Adair? Had the Adair house not been a captivity or a hiding
place for her but a hothouse wherein an exquisite bloom had
lavishly flowered? "You put a hen up to herself for a while
and she gets juicy: the longer you keep her up the juicier she
gets," is an old saying.

Nature—first fire and then something pulling her, some call
coming to her, something magnetizing her—turned her out of
her closet and drew her by night to the Thicket. Whatever it
was—looking for Mr. de Persia in her obsession with him, or
fate, or what—she went. And there she had come upon a wondrous sight.

But before I get to this, let me go back to Ace and Addis.

7

The Sunken Locomotive

All that's known is that Addis came out of the Church Orphanage up in Longview. That Ace had gone up to Longview after Addis and brought him home on the train, asked his friend and coworker the engineer to stop it in front of the house, Ace and Addis sitting in the engine, waving—and then Ace handed Jewel the little boy out of the window of the locomotive. Addis was just three, poor adopted boy, poor orphan, somebody's dream, dream son; killer son, thief son; saint son.

But Ace always stayed a little away from Addis. Wonder who Addis' parents were? he would ask. Why *we* are, Ace. No, Jewel, he'd answer. Addis is not born of you and me. I don't care, Jewel would say. Addis is *my* son. Jewel could make up a son out of Addis, but Ace couldn't.

And Ace had one chance to make a son of his own in his wife Jewel. He was in her once, stabbing quickly like a sting, and in pain and in a blind violence he had never known before, all awkward and wrong and seeming unnatural, spurting his seed everywhere like precious grain scattered away and lost—*misspent* is truly the word. Both virgins, that was their only time together. She ran from him and tore at her hair. Had he so hurt her? She became suddenly like a witch, screeching at him that he was dirty and sinful. *Sin!* He couldn't reason with her. From then on Jewel would dart back from him as if he had burnt her. He waited. His bridal flesh untouched, his young man's juices flooding him, his flesh ached. He waited, thinking, "Today . . . today she'll be ready and want me and call me and I'll go where she is and she will be lying there, open, calling me into her. I'll keep myself ready, the body of a bridegroom, my secret, and I'll wait for that golden day. Jewel will turn and change and be ready."

So Ace kept himself back, in waiting, ripe-to-bursting, vigorous and brimming, tight as a swollen pod, until that day. But that day never came. When Ace would come home from the roundhouse for noon dinner and ask Jewel to lie down and rest with him she'd answer, "There's something wrong with a man that'll come home to eat noon dinner and think of—all that. There's something wrong with you, Ace. You ought to see the doctor." "But you're my wife," Ace said. "Can't a man just lay down with his wife after dinner and . . . rest with her?" "There's no 'rest' in you, Ace. You wouldn't rest—nor let me. In the middle of the day, in the daylight—that's wrong." "But you say the same at night. You say it's wrong at night, too."

"To have—*that*—always on your mind is wrong. I told you that a hundred times. Every day, now, at noon, when you come home, all I hope for is that you won't feel that way today. I pray for you, Ace. I say, Lord, give him some rest from this wickedness in him. Give Ace some peace! Quieten Ace's . . . carnality; quieten him . . . ease him, oh Lord!"

"What a burden I lay on your soul, Jewel. Maybe I am wicked. I hurt you so much, I worry about it all the time now. At the roundhouse I say, 'what is wrong with me that I cause Jewel so much concern? What have I done?' And I'm so ashamed."

"I pray for you, Ace."

"All this time and you won't come close to me. At first, when you cried and ran from me, I said all right, Jewel.

You're young, just a girl, and scared; I'll wait. And I've never been able to get back to you. Why? Why? What happened?"

"You won't stop. You won't rest. I'm not like you . . . that way. You won't let me alone. You make me feel so . . . tainted. When I see you coming down the railroad track, home from the roundhouse, at noon or at the end of the day, I have that feeling that I can't stand in myself . . . when I just see you coming, even at a distance. I'm scared, I'm scared. And when you get close to me . . . no, no . . . it's ugly, it's wrong, it's against God. If I make you feel that way, then I am a sinner, and your temptation, Ace; and I don't know what we'll ever do, unless you change."

"Time is passing away. And I'm your husband. I need you, Jewel."

"You're a fine man, but that's a sin to think always of your body."

"You're the best Christian God ever created. You're too good for me. I'm just a no-good sinner. I'm weak, you're strong. I don't deserve you. I'll be better. You're hard to live up to, but I'll try to live up to you, Jewel. Just help me, and just give me time. You are my rock and my foundation. Guess I'd be in the gutter, with all my sinful cravings, if it wasn't for you. But I can't help asking you that didn't you know when we married that I would want to do that to you? Don't you know that I have something to give you, over and over, all through our life together. Didn't I show you once? If it's so wrong, then I swear to God I don't know what to do because I can't forget wanting to do that to you. I just can't put it out of my mind. It gets so strong in me that I'm afraid I will do something terrible if I don't let this feeling in my body have its way. You little . . . hot devil. You want me to do it and you know it! Don't you? Hanh? Hanh? Here, take it, let me! Let me! . . .

"What have I done? Oh Lord what have I done to you my own precious Jewel? God forgive me, I'm so ashamed, I'm so ashamed! I am corrupt and vile like the Bible says, and I don't know what to do. I couldn't stop! I hate myself. I hate my feelings. I hate my groins. Do you hear me Jewel? I swear to you I never touched a woman until I married you. I never sinned. How can a pure, sweet, Christian good woman like you cause a man to feel such feelings as I do toward you? It's something I cannot understand . . . and it's my cross to bear . . .

"All right, my own Jewel, my own wife, I'll be better; I'll change. And I promise you that I will never come after you again. That I will wait until you come to me. I wouldn't hurt you for anything in this world. You are a saint. Don't you know that? Hanh? God has given me a saint for a wife, and my temptations must have been put on me by the devil to try to smut up God's own saint. I will never do that! I'd kill myself first, before I'd ugly up something pure and good as you are. Now . . . now there. Don't ever be afraid of me again. Because I cross my heart and promise you in God's name that I will never hurt you again."

"My little son. *My* son. He is my redeemer. He'll make everything all right."

So no tenderness was given Ace for so long that he just died within himself. Poor Ace! So solemn and devout in his chastity. Saint Ace! His wife made a jack-offer out of him—when he got to where he couldn't stand it any longer. He touched himself for a while, but that only confirmed, in his poor soul, what Jewel had said about him, that he was a sex fiend. Finally he became a holy man, sitting off in the woods by himself. He became a sort of saint—chaste, penitent, silent.

And then he started drinking. He drank to ease his hurting and to help renounce his flesh, granting now that it was of the devil, as Jewel had declared. He drank to quell his temptations and to soothe his terrible lonesomeness. For a long time he drank his red whiskey back in the woods in the late afternoon after work. Then he took the bottle home and hid it in the well house after work. Under the stars, he drank. Through the window he could see Addis on Jewel's lap as she dressed him for bed; or, sitting behind the well house with his warm whiskey and his broken heart, suffering his vile sinner's guilt bitter as gall, he could hear Jewel reading to the little boy who (in his quiet stupor of liquor) seemed to be like the child Jesus. And when they sang together *"This Is My Father's World"* or *"From Greenland's icy mountains, from India's coral strand, where Afric's sunny fountains roll down their golden sand,"* he cried softly there in the darkness, for more than he could ever know.

Finally, he took the bottle to the roundhouse, to work, hidden in his lunch pail. He drank among the steaming engines; steam, like sweat, ran down their black sides. Somewhere within himself he did not care and wanted to die. But he went on switching the engines, standing against their black sides on a little step as they, bell tolling, moved slowly on to the turned track into their repair stall.

Had the runaway locomotive been an accident, as some said? Nobody knows whether it caught fire, exploded, went amok and charged like a maddened animal into the earth with poor Ace caught at its side; or whether Ace, berserk with whiskey and wanting to die, bound to the side by his own hand, reached in and pulled the throttle full steam. When the locomotive suddenly rushed through the wall, flinging, like a mail pouch, the engineer free, and living to try to figure what happened, who had given it full ahead? It had seemed, the engineer said later, that Satan had got hold of the throttle and the locomotive became all roaring fire, an inferno, a blasting furnace. From the ground where the engineer was thrown he said he saw for an instant in the holocaust the figure of Ace against the side of the engine—was he clinging to it or was he bound to it? was he waving one arm as if beckoning?—riding it down as it plunged and burrowed its spinning wheels, sending rockets of livid fire into the air as it thrust into the ground. And then he saw the side of the roundhouse fall and the roof slide down and fold over that—as if to cover over Ace in the locomotive. Ace was only cinder burnt up in the infernal flame, cremated in the locomotive, his urn. His consumed body had become the very cinders of the locomotive. He had lost his most golden days. He never gave his man's beautiful sweet passion. He never knew his natural joy. He lost his bloom. He withered. Poor Ace! He lost his star of hope that once hung over him. He drank his red whiskey and suffered the sadness of manhood, the sorrows of fatherhood. In his turned and soured manhood, spoiled and befouled, he was a part of the broken circuit of nature: he could not continue himself.

Jewel mourned and told Addis that his father had died in an accident in the roundhouse, and began to get Ace's railroad pension, little as it was. Addis asked no questions and he saved his wondering. He was five.

Once, at the roundhouse under which he now lay in his sunken tomb and which lay over him like a grand monument, he had almost had a woman. A Mexican woman! She had tormented him, hiding back behind the roundhouse, pulling her dress up to squat in the bushes to let the men watch her. But he would not give in. He knew he could have her. Mexican women loved it, he'd heard. And this one, especially. The men at the roundhouse talked about her, how she loved it. They'd had her back in the bushes and at night when she'd come to the roundhouse. Jim Fuller had had her standing up in an empty freight car. "She fucks like a man!" he told the others. He leaned her against the side of the car and fucked her standing up. "She gave it right back to me," he swore. "Goddam, she nearly tore it off me," he told the men. "And she kept whispering 'don't, oh don't, that hurts!'" Ace felt weak and shook with desire. If the men all had the Mexican woman together, taking turns, why couldn't he join them? They'd go back to her, each in his turn, to the dark corner where she lay on a pile of old newspapers, with her dress pulled up to her chin. Nobody could see anything, only feel. It would be perfect for him it, it would be secret and in the dark and he would not be guilty because he was not alone. The other men made it seem all right. He would do it!

The night he came back to the roundhouse, he felt a surge

of lust in him that made him shake all over and feel hot and whispery and dangerous and bold—he'd do anything to get a piece of *pussy*—he would say the word aloud like the men did, he didn't care. *Pussy!* He could smell it, what he hadn't had for so long, and he imagined touching the Mexican woman's *pussy* in the darkness. He would do everything he wanted to her, in her and outside her. In the dark! There in the darkness to have it all for yourself, warm and soft and in your hand—grabbed—like catching something alive in the dark all his own and giving, opening to him, giving back what he gave, doing it *with* him, wanting it, not fighting it, not turning away, *giving and wanting*. He would take his time. He was so starving! He would be wicked, then, like Jewel said he was. Carnality! Well, she was right. He was carnal and sinful and possessed by lust. *Fuck!* The word when he whispered it ran through his whole body and his cock leapt to it and jumped in his trousers like a frog. He would *fuck* the Mexican woman until he came and came inside her warm *pussy*. Oh Lord it had been so long. He drank his whiskey.

It was time. "She's back there," Jim Fuller told them (there were four men). "We'll draw straws. Shortest first." Ace would die if he was first. He couldn't be the first to do it. But it was Fuller who drew the shortest. He went back, looking dark faced like a murderer, into the darkness. In the gloom of the hot roundhouse, the dark engines seethed and purred and softly snorted, their smell was heavy and sexual, oozing odors of moist iron and slightly acrid steam that bit the lips and stung the tongue like the taste of a woman's heat. The men were almost solemn in their waiting. They said nothing and stood apart. The whole roundhouse was filled with sex, Ace felt. He trembled. He turned aside and drank. He was next, after Jim Fuller. In the low hissing shadow, he thought he could hear, once, the Mexican woman cry out as Jim Fuller *fucked* her. Oh what was this pain, he thought, this pain of man and woman! *Carnality!* If only he could be free of this pain, this hunger. He suddenly felt despair and without salvation and he walked a few steps toward the dark place of flesh where Jim Fuller was now growling out in a low murmur of cursing and pain, and stopped, now sobbing, and without mercy or hope or light, and he couldn't! he couldn't! he couldn't! And oh God he wanted to die, what was this life, this world? He was a husband and he had a wife and he couldn't harm that. He couldn't! He struggled and suffered. Then he turned and walked away, looking back once to see the dim, shaken-looking figure of Jim Fuller slowly coming out of the darkness, and in that moment he felt the sorrow and the tenderness and the lostness of mortality, of poor human beings, and *carnality, carnality,* oh *carnality.* What had changed everything? What had so deeply touched him, what spirit moving through the dark roundhouse? Jim looked changed, too, as though through the heat of flesh he had been redeemed of something. Ace went away, out of the roundhouse, into the night of stars. He walked the railroad tracks home.

In his room in the darkened house, he fell on his knees by his bed and cried, "Oh Lord forgive me and help me, I don't know what I'll do. If I don't have something tender, I believe I'll die." He stayed on his knees a long time, his head in his wet hands dripping with tears and saliva and mucus, as though what he had not given to the Mexican woman was now flooding out of him. He fell into some kind of trance of relief and exhaustion and unutterable sadness until the call of an owl in the nighttime shook him; and he rose and fell on his bed, asleep in his Switchman's overalls.

None of the men ever mentioned that night at the roundhouse, and Ace went on his way, waiting but hopeless. He knew he had become totally impotent since the night of the Mexican woman. He was untouchable and unarousable now, slack and unthickening, only a numb flap of skin, cold there, dead, where once he had been hot and mighty.

Except for supper with Jewel and Addis, he was alone and apart; he did not speak. What did he feel about his wife in name only, about his son in name only? Who could know? He

seemed to have no feelings at the supper table. Did he hate
them? Did he blame Addis? Who could tell? Ace seemed like
a drugged man at the supper table. Only Jewel spoke and
that was in a more or less constant stream of talking to the
boy: "Eat this. Isn't that good? Don't do that, now. Want
some more? Th-a-at's right! Sweet boy, sweet Addis Adair!"
Did he flinch when she used his name on the boy? What in
God's name was he feeling? Would anybody ever know?
Jewel didn't seem to care at all. She was in her heaven of
mothering the boy, of tending a son. And Addis was dark and
stern and silent, joyless, sometimes gazing deeply and darkly
at Ace, dark eyes fastened on him. What did Addis feel, what
was the boy thinking? This sad divided family—what would
draw them together, what would make them a family, take
away this curse that separated them? He slept in the back
room and heard Jewel singing at the piano to Addis, *"The
voice that once o'er Eden breathed,"* and he saw the moon
through the window and the vast Texas sky and the cold
stars. What is manhood? he thought. He would go away somewhere and get his man's strength back. He would be free and
refreshed and his man's vigor would juice back into him like
sap. And he would lengthen and fatten and stiffen, he would
be firm and rooted again in his manhood like a tree. But
where, where would he go, so frail now and so tired he felt
now. He was so scared. He felt himself in a trance of fear and
exhaustion. He would wake as tired as when he went to bed.
Whiskey would give him the morning strength he couldn't
find in himself.

He stumbled on the ties now, as he walked on the railroad
tracks to the roundhouse. He thought he had a vision on the
railroad tracks. It was of Jesus, the gentle comforter, who
walked on the railroad ties with him and spoke from the Gos-
pels the part that said, "Come unto me, ye who are heavy
laden." Ace walked a ways with the gentle man and heard
him say the other words, "Take my yoke upon you and learn
of me." Your yoke, your yoke, he murmured, filled with brim-

ming love for his companion of the railroad tracks, and, faint in his heart and in his head whispered, "Take my yoke, O Lord, my yoke."

Now in the ruptured and blasted ground, under the ruin of the roundhouse, lay the sweet cinders of Ace Adair, sunken in his urn of dark iron, in an engine of violence. O what was he dreaming, Ace Adair, in his sunken locomotive? In his Inferno? Fatherhood? Orphanage? Was his son's orphanage forever a mystery? Unless, like a prophecy, Addis' hidden true father would walk into the town out of the deep wilderness and announce himself, proclaiming his fatherhood of Addis, bestowing upon him his real name, and sonhood and parentage like a great prize, and redeeming Ace of his everlasting burden. Wouldn't Addis be overjoyed to accept his true father? To run and embrace his father and walk all through the town and countryside of Rose River bottom, clasping his father's shoulder, introducing him to everybody? *My father!*

Another man's son? Whose? This infernal question would be forever stopped in Ace's brain and taken off his tongue, spewed out of his mouth forever, what was haunting him in his unquiet entombment. What had been Ace's obsession as he drank his red whiskey by well house or roundhouse was the riddle, the unanswered torment of Addis Adair's orphanage. Where did this boy come from who took my wife away from me? What, O Lord, will I do with this little boy? he thought. How can I be Addis' father *when I'm not.* And how can I help find his father for him? were the questions that obsessed poor Ace's brain in his troubled death as they had tormented him in his suffering life while he sat and turned the bottle to his lips dreaming of restoring Addis' father to him. If he were able, he would go out like a knight on a quest for Addis' father as if for the Holy Grail. Could he find him, through whatever feats or ordeals he would have to endure, whatever riddles solved, he would bring him back in love and joy and that would surely be the greatest gift he could ever give to Addis: his *father!* And it would restore Jewel to him, to Ace Adair her husband, her bridegroom, her chaste and impotent bridegroom.

Roaring like a great chariot, with Ace pressed against its side, it spun its monstrous wheels, tearing open the earth, and sank headfirst. A wall of brick fell over it and then the roof fell over all that. And that was Ace's death and the destruction of the roundhouse. As the switch engine was driven into the ground, nose-first, the smokestack was bent back like a plume or the mane of a racing horse, or some immense snout; and the strange shape lay on the earth now quite like a piece of coppery wood, lacy with rust, as the only sign of the sunken locomotive. Over it, where the brick wall, now like sod, and glass roof had fallen, grew wilderness vines, blooming and ensnarled and trembling with snakes and dragonflies. It was a ruin of grandeur, this romantic ruin which was Ace's tomb. It was a hothouse of teeming growth and bloom, filled with wild flowers and ferns, orchids and delicate-petaled blooms, steeping in the rank heat and humus, the rich odor of soil and seed and mulch. In its romantic beauty it might have been the funeral monument to a hero, the mausoleum of a great prince. Yet under—somewhere—lay the gentle, unused Ace Adair, Switchman for the Neches, Brazos and Sabine Railroad, and broken-hearted husband and bewildered pseudofather, driven into the earth as if from some exploding comet.

The body of Ace Adair, with its tortured spirit crying to be liberated into the light, lay under the ruin of the collapsed roundhouse. Who would come to lift this spirit into the free light—this saint who suffered the torments of lust—the thorn in his flesh—and who took on the image of the sinner in his own eyes—who rode the locomotive down to dust, fallen into confusion over desire and purity and gone down in a godforsaken muddlement, a blind destruction, willing that his beautiful sensuality be ruined and lost to nature, burnt out to cold cinder? Who would salvage and reconcile the querulous Spirit of Ace? When would his reconciler come out of the shadows and put his soul to rest?

8
The Saint of
The Clothesline

If someone had told Addis Adair what he looked like, they'd have said: not tall, small-bodied but hard-muscled, broad-shouldered, lean legs longer than you'd expect for the rest of his body, dark complexion, black black hair that curled at his neck; and a look of devoutness, of solemness on his face. He had wandered for a while, in some kind of lust, sadness and joy—all combined in him and moving him on. Most of all he wanted his youth, wanted it for his own, to handle as he pleased, as he felt driven to, or just to have it (his youth) and let it alone, like a member of his body. He was a runaway from what threatened his youngness, his beautiful secret, so that he could keep it and use it in its own time. For some reason, in some way that he could not understand, Jewel was threatening something very private in him. "God guide me," he prayed, "and help me and look over me as I go."

Lately he had realized how deep his feelings were and how deep his needs were. He did not want to lose the days of his youth, his precious days that were *his* and would never come again. It seemed to him that anyone who would spoil or foul those precious days, tender and hurting, would be truly evil, would be harming something sacred.

There was the sense of having all the time in the world and yet very little. He was not going to be Jewel's prisoner any longer. A personal feeling, a turned-in secret, very intimate, came upon him, touching him very deeply and blindly hurting him.

As he went down the railroad tracks that night, he felt a mixture of excitement and heartbreak. What was this life? He had to go into it, to find out. What did it mean, this strange thing—*life*—that had its restless sources like springs in the ground and that had nothing to do with lifeless places. You could feel it in the soil: here you could put your hand and feel coldness, aridness, dumb clay: here you could feel energy and quickness and struggling and richness; here you planted, here the green grew. So he was looking for one of the centers of life, where life clustered and went deep and rich, and already he knew that there would be hurt and confusion and despair, for where deep life was, there was turmoil as well as peace. He sought life—he knew that was why he was leaving.

And walking on the railroad tracks—the train was now gone and never came that way again on those rusted, weed-covered ties and rails—he thought, for the millionth time, it seemed, of his strange poor lost other father, Ace. The older he got, though Ace had gone by the time he was only five, the more vividly, the more intensely he remembered Ace. Ace had been a kind of ghost, a spirit moving over and with him, through his life. Ace! If he had known Ace! He felt, now, that Ace was going with him, traveling down the railroad tracks, off into the dark beyond, into the dark unknown. As he had grown up, though Jewel had kept him closely to her and away from the world, Addis had gathered word of Ace from this one and that one who once in a while came on the place. And, most of all, a lingering presence of Ace gave him a sense of the man—some instinctive knowledge, primitive and of the heart and genitals and blood. The man Ace, his other father, had entered Addis' spirit and lived in him, dwelt in his heart. The sadness and doubt around his terrible death were now relieved forever, as though he, the violently buried Ace, had been lovingly borne up from his tomb of confoundment, recon-

ciled and brought to peace. And the love of Addis had done
it. Addis had come upon a little oval photograph of Ace no
larger than a silver dollar (he could hold it in the palm of his
hand, cup his hand over it), with the bill of his Switchman's
cap turned devilishly to the side, over one ear, with a look of
tenderness and hurt on his stern face. Addis had stolen the
Switchman's cap off the nail it had hung on all these years,
and he had stolen the photograph and felt he was taking Ace
for his own, into his life forever, as his eternal companion of
sorrow and orphanage. He always carried the photograph in
his pocket in a Prince Albert tobacco can, along with a few
other precious possessions: a small glass swan from a box of
candy crackers long ago, and a rainbow in full color on a piece
of isinglass framed by cardboard which came from a loaf of
Wonder bread. The Prince Albert can was also his money
wallet (he had left with ten dollarbills and two quarters,
which he had saved for this time.

One thing he most loved, and it was his secret, was to walk
on wire. He would never know, never even questioned, why
he was so anxious to learn to walk really well, barefooted on
a piece of clothesline. It was as natural for him as wanting to
swim. He had, early on, found that he could do it quite easily. He had used Jewel's clothesline stretched between the
washhouse and the tree near it and had fallen a few times,
but got up and tried again. He had never thought any more
about this feat than that it gave him joy and made him feel
free. When he left, the only thing he took from the place was
Jewel's clothesline. He had learned to walk on this length of
wire and it had become dear to him, very personal; it knew
his feet, and his toes knew the wire, had grown callouses
against its bruising hurt. He had to have it. He substituted another for it and Jewel would never know the difference.

As he walked down the railroad track, with the Switchman's cap on his head, the coil of wire around his shoulder (it
was so personal to him and went away with him as close as a
part of his body) and the little photograph of Ace in his pocket

in the tin box, he said good-bye to the town of his imprisoned childhood and his orphaned lonesomeness. And to Jewel. He loved her and he would miss her, but he could not give his life to her. She was not his mother; and lately he had kept telling her please to go lightly with her protestations of motherhood, that she was not his mother. He had had to do this and had not meant it to be cruel. He just had to have it straight and clear. Jewel wept and wept; all day again and through the night he heard her sobbing. Poor thing—she had had only him and now she would have nothing. But he couldn't stand it, being out of life, or not knowing what the world was, being in a prison with Jewel. He was fifteen and had to have his life for himself, had to have his bitter orphanage for his own, to have it and to understand it and to take it into the world. Jewel would get along. In fact, she would be better off without him around to torment her by making her have to pretend she was his mother, and she would have more peace without having to hear his denials that stabbed her with heartbreak. Now she would have to face life's reality and accept the truth. She would have suffocated him with possessiveness, strangled him with her tormented mother's affection. He couldn't breathe. He was an orphan. He belonged to no one he knew. Somewhere were his parents, unless they were dead. He was tired of trying to imagine his true mother and father, as tired as poor Jewel was—she'd see, now that she was relieved of him—of having to make up a son out of him. He was an orphan. And now he was free. Parentage, kin, *bloodkin,* what did they mean? He was outside all that; he had none of it. He was alone. And now the time had come for him to declare his natural aloneness, his purity, his oneness.

The Texas moonbeams fell over his face and shone coppery on the rusted tracks and silvery on his ring of wire. Ace! scattered brokenhearted in the roundhouse ground, your true friend, but not your son, is going away. Ace! your everlasting companion who loves you and whose love you never got to know (would it have changed you? would it have saved your

life, if you had known the love that I would come to have for
you? No. How sad that you would have to die for me to love
you!) Ace! who died for me. Come away with me now. Ace!
who died because of me, follow me and be my guide. We will
go to wonderful places and have a marvelous adventure. I
hope you know how you've touched my life, how you now
hold my life and my dreams. I understand you. You have to
be an orphan to understand a sonless father, a wifeless husband, to understand a lonesome person. Funny that he felt he
was leaving Jewel to be with Ace, to go away with him, companions in freedom and adventure and loneliness.

Now he was leaving a strange and hidden life that Jewel
had made for him back in that darkened house. She had kept
him away from everybody. Fewer and fewer visitors came.
He would sit on the leaning well house and look out over the
place. Standing up, he looked out as far as he could see. He
felt strange and odd as he grew older. Very early he knew
about sexual power, the fierceness of something, some yearning, some excited longing that he had felt touching him in his
hidden personal place, lifting him and blindly hurting him,
that seemed to be the center of himself, as if it were his heart
there under his thigh, drawing to it most everything that happened and affecting most everything he did. This feeling was
something to have to go around with and he knew, for himself, would be with him always, now that it had come. He
loved it and feared it, wanted it and didn't.

But what was this sadness over him as he went on? It was
for Jewel. As his eyes opened and he saw things more clearly
—as if his eyes were coming into focus—he saw this peculiar
woman. She never let him go; wherever he was she would
suddenly be there; he grew up at her feet, knees, side. It was
then, when he was around eleven, that he began to escape

from her, to hide, to flee. What was this thing in him that
drove him to run away, to break loose? From then on, his
memory was of Jewel's voice calling him. Addis! Addis! Come
here! When he finally came to her, crawling out of a hiding
place or coming back from where he had started—sometimes
even on the road, a foot even on the road that ran near the
house, to go on down it and away, to go alone or find the
Gypsies that occasionally passed by and join them, the flashing Gypsy girls and the sly and sultry men. And when he
would come back to Jewel she'd grab him to her and cry and
clutch him until she dug her fingernails into his flesh. How
she held him! It worried and scared him. It made him shudder, hold himself hard so as not to fight loose, it made him feel
caught and he could feel the heat rise in him; he felt angry
and he was afraid, as he grew older and stronger, that he
would thrust Jewel away from him and throw her down.
Something warm was in Jewel, though, that often held him to
her as she clutched at him—what he was trying to turn away
from was pulling him back. When he had finally broken away,
he was trembling and felt personal, secret. He had scarcely
seen another woman. The black woman Mary Bird came
sometimes to help wash, and all day he would watch her in
the well house. She was about thirty, he guessed. And once in
a while girls that lived way up the road and back in the trees
would be on the road—he'd catch their silent figures going
down the road. Once he almost followed them, to go home
with them, where he imagined they would all sit together at
the kitchen table and eat together; and it would be warm and
happy. But even then he knew he would have to leave them;
he would always have to go away, to leave. He was an orphan. Addis! Come here! the voice called. But he would not.
He would keep himself away and he would not touch anybody, only himself when he had to, when he was startled
and overcome by the special pain of himself, when only to
move a little was to break open something ready to burst in

him, something clogged and strutted and heavy to bear, and out it would burst, an explosion out of himself, a miracle, a mystery, and an ecstasy.

Well, he had gone on that night, on the railroad tracks under the white moon of Texas, on away. When he passed the roundhouse ruin, tenderness rushed through him and he whispered, "Good-bye, Ace, that I never knew, in the roundhouse grave, hello Ace that came back to me and now lives in me and goes with me, the new Ace that came to me a long time ago and now goes with me. Good-bye Ace, hello Ace."

For Ace had really become a living presence in him and around him. Did Ace have to die to enter Addis' life? Why did he have the assurance, the feeling that Ace had *had* to die in order to be with him? It was one of the things he wanted to find out about, one of the many things, but probably the most important of all, that he wanted to talk to somebody about. In a way, he was not running away, but after somebody to talk to, to have conversations with, to ask questions, for a while before he would have to run away again, even from them, who had talked closely and lovingly with him. He was so used to silence. In the last strange and anxious year, he and Jewel would go day upon day without speaking hardly at all, and on some whole days they had not spoken a word. He sometimes said some words aloud to hear himself speak, and then his voice sounded hollow and strange and not his own. His loneliness was sometimes almost unbearable, but it was his to bear, he had grown up knowing this, and he had Ace and drew the sense of Ace close to him, almost like prayer, and felt—well, he guessed—*fathered* and consoled. And how strange for him to feel that he, fatherless boy, had become a kind of father to Ace! He would take care of Ace, protect him, give him consolation, *father* him; and again, in this new light, in the light of this new discovery, this insight, he asked himself, *what is a father, anyway?* Can somebody be both son and father?

He put up his clothesline and walked it on street corners in the little towns, or in fields and meadows. He made two folding poles and strung the wire between them. In time he had acquired a worn satin top hat and a pair of old cowboy boots soft as the side of a cow, with small shining silver stars still bright on them. He walked the wire at open-field church meetings, outdoor celebrations. He lived on the contributions watchers put in a bucket. For many months he wandered and traveled, earning his way on his wire. He discovered that he had a hold over people, that he could hold them in thrall. He felt a power. Some thought he was the Second Coming, Jesus on a clothesline walking it like He did water. Others were a little afraid of him, he looked so dark, and in his black frazzled satin hat he looked scary and threatening and sensual in his somber, brooding kind of beauty. Was he a Gypsy? What was he? In his power and dominion over his witnesses he nevertheless estranged people—which was his nature and what he meant to do—so there was no problem of anybody invading his privacy. He was a lone figure treading a wire like a bird or a dark angel, a dusky moth, something winged over the towns; and so he moved on.

Once in a while he was told to move on by a suspicious little town. But nobody made passes at him, whispered suggestive words to him or sent him obscene notes, although his attraction to them was sexual. But they turned it into something pure. His soul, his deeper purity drew them to him. What people apparently felt was his dark contradicting purity, his holiness; and he became a kind of saint figure in the Panhandle—exactly why, nobody could explain. But his passionate performance would convert more than corrupt, seduce to penitence more than to prurience, for some mysterious reason.

People brought him food and they brought gifts, and he endured and went on.

Yet he never opened his mouth, this speechless wire dancer, this strangely appealing saint of the clothesline in the dry desertland, on the dusty mesas of the Panhandle; and nobody tried to make him talk. His performance was executed in absolute hushedness. Addis was like a hypnotist. His audience was enraptured and, too, utterly hushed. This silent balancing figure hovered over Texas, as much aboveground as on the ground—a hushed flight not of clouds but of ground mists.

For a year he wandered and performed. He slept in missions, in fields, under bridges, all through the western desertland in the dry red-dirt and black-dirt windy towns blown over by red winds and black winds. He never made a friend.

Ace dies

Addis never makes friend

wandered for a year

9
Faithful Jake

Word came of a passionate man named Cleon Peters moving through the Piney Woods country carrying in a screen-covered box a white rattlesnake with ruby-colored diamonds on its back. It was the time of the discovery of oil in the fields of East Texas, around 1930.

It was said that this Cleon Peters, a snake preacher and healer, was repeatedly getting an insistent Call to change his profession. He had been a Second Coming preacher who had grown tired of prophesying what continued to embarrass him by never coming and, confounded dead in his tracks in a halt at the fork of his life's crossroads, waited for his Crossroads Decision on his knees all one night outside Sour Lake. Cleon Peters seemed nailed to the cross of intersection of two roads —fixed there, he said, "where time and eternity intersect." The question was whether he was going to be led toward Time or Eternity. A crowd stood by waiting to find out with him, to witness the spectacle of him hearing the final decree of his Call. Near early morning he heard it and was led to his decision by the Lord—toward oil. Reborn, Cleon Peters got right up off his knees and took the road leading to East Texas oil country with hundreds following him. "Follow me folks, goin to the Promised Land. Glorious times are ahead for us." he proclaimed. "You all who have witnessed this red-letter night of my life goin to be the first to get filthy rich from oil on your property."

In a brief sort of sermon delivered on foot as he walked—and in what was the last breath of Cleon Peters, the end-of-the-world preacher—he said he felt that he could help people whose home in heaven he'd secured for them, blessed assurance, by now giving them some earthly security through finding oil on their property. Where once he had been the Savior of the Piney Woods, a territory which he had combed through for souls to save, he was now going to become the King Of The Oilfields and comb through that same territory for oil. He anointed himself "Oil King," and moved on fast, leading a good-sized flock. He had the technique for salvation. All he had to do was convert it over. And he had *faith*. For anything, no matter what it was, you had to have *faith*. Anybody who *believed* could do all things—take up serpents, receive deadly poison and not die, cast out devils, speak in tongues—and find oil. God had been Cleon Peters' friend through physical risk and spiritual tribulation in a world of things not seen: obedience, humility, faith. Now He would help Oil King in a world more substantial—and more visible: oil derricks, oil pumps, drilling tools, cash money.

All that part of Texas was roused up and flocking here and there. The towns were startled because of the sensational rumor that everybody in the counties of East Texas was walking, eating, and sleeping on top of about forty million dollars. It was the time of great flux and change, though it was not the kind of change that Oil King had once foreseen and got people ready for. Because a man who blew in a wildcat well announced that he was positive there was a huge black lake of oil stretching under five counties, such a pandemonium started you'd have thought he had proclaimed the end of the world. Thousands of people ran, whirled, tumbled and collided, dug up rows of turnip greens, ran through the streets with dishpans full of dirt, yelling oil! oil! and the news slipped into Oil King's ear as though it were a key to wind up a mechanism in

him that sent him prancing like a high strutter into his old
snake-haunted territory with his good news of the coming of
oil glory.

The fortunes of Oil King began right away with his discovery well Number One. Number One had been a true O.K.
from the Lord on Oil King's new life's work. It had not blown
in at all, was not a gusher but an oozer—on his knees, nose to
the ground, he had sniffed, prayed, envisioned and be-
seeched: and lo! he had damp knees. Oil! Oil King's whirlwind success firmly established him overnight in oil country.
The big-time oil companies sent their geologists with college
educations to try to buy him out, but Oil King turned a deaf
ear on them. "Come back next Tuesday, big deal from the
university," he said. "You got your degree, I got my knees.
And the Lord's geology—*faith*."

Number One was famous all over the county and people
came from miles around to gaze at it. It was in the yard of
what had been a poor dirt-farm family, the McCrackens.
There it was, pumping away, with zinnias blooming around
it and blinking colored lights and strings of bells strung up
and down the thrusting pump. Number One was used by Oil
King for demonstrations to attract lessors from the neighbor-
ing towns, and even far away in farther counties, farms, and
pastures. That Number One was so used by Oil King delighted
the McCrackens, who sat proudly on the front porch in swing
and rocking chair. Eula McCracken and her daughter Murtice dressed up for the demonstration. Eula had on a hat she
had bought by telephone from Neiman-Marcus in Dallas after
seeing a picture of it in a newspaper; it had come by parcel
post in an elegant box. On her dinner-ring finger was a big
sapphire the size of a bird's egg. "We didn't do a thang," she
told the visitors. "Lord put it in the ground, Oil King took it
out. Now we're rich. Please don't trod on my zinnias."

Murtice would wear a variety of chiffon gowns with big
bird figures or huge sunflowers or enormous palm trees printed
on them—sometimes she would change as many as three times

in one afternoon; and she smoked her cigarettes. They said in town that she broke the scale at the drugstore at 229, but that was just a nasty crack, Murtice commented. "Anyways, I'll buy you ten of those things if that'll make you happy," she told the owner of the store. "I own one third of Number One and I'm goin to live in Dallas in a mansion with servants. Get outa this crappy little town."

But Mack McCracken just drank his good Bourbon, gliding in the porch swing mumbling, "Five thousand barrels a day." Now the foreman at the mill could go fuck himself.

On the Cadillac parked in the dirt yard sat two Dominick hens. A bird dog lay in the shade under it.

"Hey, Murtice," Chuck Snyder, the football hero, called. "Lend me five." Chuck Snyder had let it be known that he got Murtice's cherry under the high school steps on Hallow-een. "A simple operation," he told. "Wasn't exactly a matter of surgery. Let's put it thataway. Anyway, I opened the gate for the male population of the whole fuckin high school."

"Papa, run Chuck Snyder off the place. He's given me a problem," Murtice said.

"Five thousand barrels a day," muttered Mack McCracken.

"Hey, Murtice"—Chuck winked and made a hidden gesture with his big finger that only Murtice could see—"take me for a ride in your Cadillac."

"Wouldn't dream of disturbin the Dominickers," Murtice answered.

Glittering with diamond buttons on his coat, diamond hat-band on his ten-gallon hat, diamond cufflinks and diamonds down his fly, Oil King would prance up and down on a plat-form by the side of Number One, ranting in his Revivalist voice. Sometimes he leapt aboard the oil pump and rode it like a bronco. "Ever time I go down, folks, Number One gushes up hundred dollars out of good ole Texas ground. Get in on it!" People came from all around to spend the day, bringing milk pails, cake pans, mason jars, and well dippers full of dirt from their land for Oil King to smell. They spread dinner on the ground and at night there were Roman Candles shot in the air, and the colored lights twinkled and swayed on Number One, and the bells rang. It was the happiest time a lot of poor folks ever knew or would remember.

Oil King had brought back together the little group who had assisted him in his Revival days, to put on a show of entertainment for prospective investors. "These folks was with me when I used to be going around Texas a-prophesying the end of everything," Oil King announced. "Now they've joined me for the beginning of things, glory hallelujah! Gonna be a new day!"

"You got the word on it, Oil King!" exclaimed rednecked and lanky Elsie Wade, who had traveled with the Show of Faith Revival, playing with her red-speckled hands the portable pump organ that folded up like a suitcase.

"Brethren, listen to Elsie Wade that's been with me through dark and daylight. We got to oil up this old world or its goan go dry. And I'm the man to find the necessary lubrication."

"'aaat's right, Oil King," chimed in the petite Xylophone Twins, Esther and Hester, as they daintily hammered a rippling sound on the little Xylophone upon which they played "Welcome Sweet Springtime" for the demonstration.

"You got the power, Oil King!" called out Arab. Arab was over seven feet tall and wore ballooning Persian pants and cowboy boots. Most of the time he stood like a statue in all his grandness so that people could gaze in awe at him. Then it came time for him to make his speech to the crowd. "Folks, I measure seven foot three inches from tip of my head to sole of my bare foot. Was borned of normal size, up in Corrigan. 'Twas at the age of twelve that for no reason at all except the will of God begun to shoot up tall as a beanstalk; and by age of fourteen had reached seven foot. The three inches come on me after that. I am in perfeck health. Eat me a chicken a day, a dozen biscuits, and drink me a gallon of sweet milk ever day that I live. Any questions?" The crowd was tongue-tied.

Arab was a good bodyguard and bouncer for Oil King, whose safety and well-being were occasionally threatened by those who felt they'd been cheated or were being addressed by a fraud. Once a man called Oil King a queer and another time he was accused by a woman who called out that he was a kneefucker. She was bounced out of the demonstration meeting by Arab, but he whispered, "Make date," and she whispered back, "Midnight behind the P.O."

Using his Evangelist's gift of the word, Oil King delivered a sermonlike speech, rousing and persuasive, on the possibility of oil in a person's backyard. It was called his Possibility Of Oil speech.

"Brothers and Sisters, I'm goin to tell you something. I used to be a rattlesnake preacher. Know what that is? That's right, lady. Probably seen me around state o' Texas in my Show Of Faith."

"I remember the rattlesnake preachers when I was just a little bitty thing, remember it clear as day," the lady sang out. "People come from miles around in their wagons to watch the spectacle and the demonstration of faith in the field across from our house. Preacher said 'twas the end of the world. We sat up half the night, mamma and papa and all of us children, scared and still, but trying to hold our faith. We sat together on the front porch and we waited and waited, not saying one word. Then we heard the tumult at the revival in the fields. And pretty soon across the railroad tracks come somebody a-running, and it was Mr. Bell that lived up back. 'God help us. God help us, Miz Polk! The preacher of faith is dead! He was bitten by the diamond rattler and dropped down dead in the pulpit! No one would lift a hand to help him. 'Tis the end of the world as was prophesied!' The congregation stampeded, the wagons all over the road and ever whichaway in the field and the dust was all over the field and rising up over the town like smoke. It was a heathen sight."

"Terrible thing." Ex-brother Cleon Peters suddenly became very sinister-looking and some dark look came over his face.

"Preacher had no faith and the snake got him. I seen it happen too. You got to have faith." Then Oil King's face lost Cleon Peters' dark look and lit up. "Well . . . I was never bit to where I couldn't throw off the poison of the serpent through my faith—thank you Lord God Jesus; and I pitched my Second Coming tent in the grass and the bitterweeds of many a field all over this blessed state. But that's all over. Come a time when I rose up out of the fields, out of the grass and the bitterweed, folded my Revival tent where I shouted and proclaimed the end of the world—to announce that this old world ain't never goan end; just gonna go on and on, gettin richer and sweeter and happier, with all the good things pourin into our laps out of the horn of plenty. What glorious times are ahead for everybody, folks!"

"Take Number One, for example. Wildcat well. Found it on my knees, and with my nose to the ground. Ain't it the prettiest thing you ever saw? Now these folks the McCrackens going to help themselves to about a half-million dollars. When Number One blew in, whole town was out here to see it. That ole wildcat just showered this town with mud and rock, all drenched in oil. Town had a celebration, everybody rollin on the ground in mud and rocks drenched in oil. A beautiful sight to see—linger forever in my memory. I want you to have that same sight, too. 'Cause we got to oil up this old world. It's going to go dry. Cain't turn much longer without any lubrication, now can it?"

"Cain't do it!" called out a voice that ran through the crowd like electricity and set on end the short hairs of the men. The magnetic sound came from a woman who had lately become a camp follower of Oil King, a clubfooted woman in a built-up shoe (some said it was a cloven hoof and that she was one of the Devil's women and a leading member of the visible and invisible evil spirits that the Devil had sent to pervert and satanize Brother Cleon Peters). Her name was Lydia and Lydia spoke with something of a lisp, which it was said was so sexy that men would get a hard-on just hearing her say

"Hoddy!" It was rumored that she was a real slut of the oil-fields when she joined up with Oil King, but that using his old powers to serve his new life, he had cast out from Lydia a devil—a humping spirit—and drove it into the oil pump of Number One: which was putting a cast-out devil to work where it could do the most good—although some of Lydia's old friends protested that. This represented a perfect example of Oil King's amazing converting powers which he so ingeniously put to work—borrowing from Peter to pay Paul, but the money stayed in the family, as he said. "No use wasting cast-out devils like those in the swine that ran over the cliff and into the sea in the Bible. A waste of swine. And the misapplication of a bunch of damn useful devils," pronounced Oil King. "O Brothers and Sisters!" he called. "I got me a dream! Goin to see the forests of Texas cleaned right out and working with oil pumps—chug chug chug all through the night and all through the daytime. I'm goin to change state of Texas! Where there are shotgun houses and one Poland china pig rootin up acorns under a live oak tree, and white leghorns roostin on the front steps, I'll bring two-story mansions."

"Tell it out, Oil King!" shouted Elsie Wade.

"You cain't let oil wait! It's waited too long. It wants to come up! I worked too long as a revivalist for something that *didn't* come. The end of the world. No more waiting! Things got to *materialize.*"

"You got the word on it!" called Arab.

"'aat's *right!*" cooed the Xylophone Twins and hammered their rippling sound on the portable Xylophone.

"Now ladies and gents, for a long time I thought our days was numbered, that we was living at the tail end o' time; end was just around the corner; any minute you'd hear that trumpet sound and it'd be curtains. Curtains for this old sad world. But now I see different. I got a new Call. Now I want to be right in the middle of it, roll and wallow in it, rub up against it, this sad old beloved sweet world."

"Speak of it!" Lydia lisped, as if she were sucking something.

"When I preached the end of the world and it didn't come
. . . I learned that *people love this world.* You know that? You
wouldn't guess it sometime, but oh, my! people do love this
old hard world. I bore a lot of disappointment. The end of the
world never come. Prayed and shouted all night, *plus* en-
dangering my physical welfare to the bite of a rattlesnake—
two inches o' hot fang—converted souls, got 'em all ready—
ever kind of good man and bad man; dope fiends, sex maniacs,
perverts, sin-ridden people—and it didn't come. Next day
bright as ever, same old situation: people and trouble. Morning, noon and night come, same as usual. Same old everyday
situation. People was so relieved world hadn't ended they gam-
bled and drunk liquor and . . . *everthing else,* harder'n ever,
they was so glad to have the world all back, to make up for
what they almost lost. Just tore up a town, so glad to have the
world back for a little longer . . . and I left town in disgrace
and the object of local ridicule. They blamed *me!* Well no
Sir! No more disappointment! No more waitin! is what I say.
Work with *this* world, the one we got here; and that's what
I say now: don't linger folks. Let Oil King get his hands in
your ground and he'll bring up oil dirt . . . you watch. Trust
in him! Go along with him; pitch in and help, even—like they
done right here with Number One. Brothers and Sisters . . .
I ask for your . . . *faith.* And may the Good Lord bless you
and keep you all the days of your life, and may the peace of
understanding come into your hearts. Amen. . . . you can
get in on it for ten dollars. Who's first and don't crowd me."

At the end of the Possibility Of Oil sermon people would
line up to come to Oil King just as they had when Cleon Peters
preached with Jake the rattlesnake—come forth to make their
confession of faith and give their lives to the Lord. Except this
time they came forth to bring their what Oil King called
"Lease Money"—ten dollars an acre to prophesy oil—and
leave their name and the location of their property. In time

Oil King would get there and give them what he called his Knee Job. Oil King therefore became one of the first independent oil men in Texas, turning Camp Grounds into Oilfields.

All this was good except that Faithful Jake, the white rattlesnake with ruby-colored diamonds on his back, was now a leftover, an orphan (he was reputed to be twelve years old and he had a magnificent rattler on him). "Although I've had me a tremendious success and am known as the Oil King of Texas, goin to make lots of folks filthy rich, must say I got a soft spot in my heart for them old days when I carried Jake around with me in his cage, demonstrating to many a troubled heart the power of faith and preparing 'em for the end of the world," Oil King mused.

No one from those parts had ever seen another snake like Jake. This deluxe creature was the only one of his kind—a ruby-backed rattler, obviously a mutated diamondback. Jake's diamonds had changed to rubies. He was a valuable serpent and would have been stolen a hundred times were it not for his deadly dangerousness.

What to do with the main prop of Show Of Faith that had broken up—the very soul of the show? Because although it was Oil King's daring faith that was the drawing card of the show—which was performed at Revivals, Camp Meetings, even street-preaching demonstrations—it was the unbiting of Jake, the powerful self-control, the amazing restraint, the dramatic power of the faith of Jake that was the very spirit of the act: *Jake's Faith.* Jake was truly blessed, truly a divine instrument, an obedient servant of the Lord, the Lord's true steward. He lived by faith. Oil King was only the medium for Jake to do his work through (flesh to be bitten or not bitten: snakebite material, as he said). Jake was the Lord's snake. Oil King was only the handler, Jake's tool, Jake's agent for salvation by faith: Jake the Christian rattlesnake.

Now poor Jake must live by faith alone, for what had he to do with Cleon Peters' new profession? Brother Cleon Peters had changed Jake's nature—from a vicious and hostile viper, striking at anything and squandering without conscience his deadly venom (it had been analyzed by a Cherokee who found it to be of triple strength in poison content and as copious as that of three snakes combined). But through Brother Peters' teaching and patient prayer Jake had changed into a disciplined creature, a thing of self-control and obedience, triumphant over self. It was Jake's faith, then, that was the drawing card for the hundreds who came to witness his Show of Faith. "I, Cleon Peters, am just the poor humble servant of a holy snake of faith. Jake is the potter, I am the clay. Give me no credit. Just consider me possible snakebite material, tha's all!"

What to do with Faithful Jake? Where does an old snake go who, if he *had* to bite, bit in great faith that he would not poison the bitten to death? God knows he tried hard not to, held back and held back until he thought he'd burst, and when he couldn't hold back any longer let go a slug, a bolt of poison, praying that it wouldn't kill Cleon Peters. It was then Peters' turn—to resist by faith, by prayer—calling on the Lord. And the Lord saved him the times Jake slipped and bit him.

Besides his faith, Jake's rubies, burning deep-fired on the broad back of his milk-white body, were just about all he had. Yet, vanity of vanities, they were of no lasting value. Each year they fell off his back into lusterless scales and, lying on the ground or on some bush, were no more illustrious than an old piece of skin. Yet Jake was blessed by the knowledge of sacrifice which came from the experience of having to give up regularly his most precious possession, the very skin off his back. His most precious possession was that which he readily gave up. Of course he had his poison, which he gave up in violence, coiling and striking, using his whole ruby-spangled body, the iron coil of himself, to thrust and shoot it out like green bullets. But he gave up his rich, deadly, and

plenteous venom only in extremes, only in moments of
radical necessity. Then Cleon Peters, stricken and poisoned,
would cry, "Praise the Lord! I have faith! In faith there is
no death! I will not die!"

But where does an old snake go? Someone had to look
after him, for he was very old and almost all his poison had
been used up—and without his threat what, then, could be
the true uses of faith that was dependent upon danger? Without a challenge, what was faith? It had to be tested. It was
almost a theological problem or perhaps a metaphysical hy-
pothesis, one that churchmen like Augustine or Origen or
Luther or Calvin might have held long disputations on, had it
been another era. But this was in the 1930s in the ratty oil-
towns of the boom fields and among people who grew up on
pea and pepper farms and saw the Devil walking in the river
bottom or sitting on the roof of an outhouse and lived by in-
disputable faith and walked with sweet Jesus their comforter
and companion in poverty and sickness and were guided by
preachers of faith and sin and redemption. But this gives you
an idea of the fundamental and historical significance of Jake,
whose rubies were a bit blurred, for age was beginning to tar-
nish them.

It was Oil King's thought to let Jake loose in the Thicket.
But how could he ever survive, a snake so old and senti-
mentalized by memory, gentled by constant use of fidelity, so
dreaming and priestly an old creature? Poor Jake. Nevertheless, it seemed that the white ruby-backed rattlesnake was
going to be put in the refuge of the Thicket—a sweet haven
for an old tired ancestor of the wilds to die in, this ancient
creature of the dust of the ground, of creation's very beginnings.

While Oil King was torn and tormented by what was the
right thing to do, it was suggested by Hester and Esther, the
sweet Xylophone Twins who had loved Jake for years, that
Oil King find a good home for the serpent where he would be
loved and given proper care by an adoring companion. Oil

King ought to advertise, leaving word and signs and ads in churches, Revival tents, in post offices, etc.

About this time a very significant event in the life of Addis Adair was happening. Just when he was so lonesome that he thought he would die, walking on a road of dust that led, it seemed, to nowhere, he saw a sign nailed to a tree which announced a special Tent Meeting in the town ahead. It was here that Addis saw what he thought was surely one of the most beautiful things in the world—Jake the white rattlesnake. Jake was lying upon the breast of a big warm man who called himself Oil King, ex-preacher, confessor to sinners and healer. It was then that Addis learned of the special powers of Jake and of the bleak future ahead of him unless someone befriended him.

And then Addis heard Oil King make his famous speech that he used to make when he was traveling around as a faith preacher with Jake. "Folks this is old Jake, and he's stung me I bet a hundred times and never laid me low. But that was when he got to where he couldn't help it; and it never laid me low. I rose up refreshed out of it every time, renewed by the power and strength of my own faith. I've seen old Jake lie up against me soft and calm as a kitten asleeping. But I know the thunder and lightning in him. Jake can strike like scissored lightning. And in him is the poisoning that can lay a man down and blow him up purple till he busts with the gall of Satan. See how he writhes! See his green eye! And all that cottony soft white mouth. You ole slippery codger. Sin lover! Coo coo coo coo coo coo!"

Addis was so drawn to the beautiful Jake that he knew he had to have him. As he started down the aisle of the crowded tent, the people turned and stared at him in his frazzled Switchman's cap, dust-covered and weatherbeaten, his old cowboy boots with the rusted stars on them, and his clothes-line coiled around his shoulder. The congregation was hushed and Oil King stopped talking and fastened his eyes on the curious figure coming up the aisle to him, walking on the sawdust, holding a ten-dollar bill in his hand.

When Addis came before Oil King's face and showed him his own forlorn and visionary face, Oil King said, "Boy, you look blue. You got somethin on your soul that's making you blue. You got some pain on you."

Addis held out the ten dollars. The tent was hushed. Oil King stared and seemed to be filling with some deep filling. And then it brimmed out of him.

"Great good God, all of a sudden seems like my youth come on me again, looking upon you. I remember my youth suddenly crawling all over me like a thousand hot tongues all over my body. I walked, I bet, a thousand miles over Texas, trying to get the crawling hot tongues of my youth off me. I'll never forget my thousand miles. I got it out on Texas. I worked out my youth on Texas, rubbed it off on a thousand miles of Texas. I got a deep feelin' you the same as I was. Like me, son, like I was."

Addis' eyes were filled with tears, and his face was covered with darkness and had a look of confusion and strife. The hand that held out the ten-dollar bill shook.

"Son, I bet you got no parents. Where's your parents? I bet you're a boy of the road. Wearin that cap. Tell me boy, where you come from, where you goin?" Oil King waited. The congregation hardly breathed, and then Oil King saw Addis' lips struggle and tremble and Addis' whole mouth strained to make words and only blew gasping breath.

"Oh God help you blue boy of the road, you caint talk. You got no words, God help you. Somebody's got to cut loose the cord that ties your tongue, like the boy in the Bible. Vow to God if I was back on the road with my old Show Of Faith I'd take you with me. Cause you belong to the Lord, in His capture some way, caint tell how; but I see the hand of the

Lord on you, and His sorrow and rejection's in your eyes. I'd
ask you to come with me and help me in my new profession,
cause God knows you could help me, you got the power, 's all
over you, beaming outa you, the power; and God knows
everbody in Texas got *boom* on their minds, anybody in
Texas owns one *inch* of ground out smellin and rootin to see
if they got oil in it; whole state's on its haunches with its nose
to the ground. You could make your fortune, become a big
man in Texas. But you're a Saint, a blue Saint, and I cain't
claim you—although my personal opinion is that all Saints
ought to be rich. They deserve it. But I swear to God above
Almighty that the Devil would strike me down if I took you
from the Lord that has seized your lonesome soul and is
savin it for some purpose I caint prophesy. Some destiny He's
put on you. I just know you're the Lord's own possession.
Couldn't take *you*. Lord has sent you here to claim old Jake.
He's yours, saint boy, the viper's yours." And when Oil King
saw a flicker of light spread over the boy's face, he said
quietly, almost like a prayer, and in a sobbed voice watery
with tears, "He don't eat much. He just dozes away most of
the day. He's old, he needs love."

And then Oil King placed the cage in Addis' hand and
asked him to kneel and take off his cap, and then Oil King
took a pitcher of drinking water and baptized Addis. The
congregation fell on its knees, and this was a still and holy moment and meant more to everybody than anybody knew, and
Addis wept and realized how he had been shut off from love,
from the love of God, in his darkness, and he thought he
heard a voice cry out from inside him words that he could
never have understood: "O that Thou shouldst give dust a
tongue to cry to Thee!": and suddenly he felt almost blinded
by a blazing light and out of the dazzling light walked toward
him two beautiful people all in white, a young man and a
young woman, and he believed it was a vision of his parents.
And then a startling thing happened to Addis. Some wild spirit
entered into him and his tongue loosened and trilled like a

bird's. Addis Adair found tongue and spoke. "We are all one family. There are no fathers and there are no sons."

When Addis rose from his baptism he seemed like a young saint or a young holy knight. And when he turned and went up the aisle with the cage in his hand, his face shone and his eyes were radiant and the people were sure that he was going on some quest of beauty and magic and wonder, and many followed him—as if they were laying down everything to follow him. And Oil King's voice intoned out, as if in some Emperor's benediction, "Go on now, holy boy. Nobody can keep you. You're meant for the road. You go on now."

Now, in the towns Addis drew greater crowds, walking his wire with Jake coiled around his neck and lying upon his breast. And he took Jake closer and closer to him, as his very own.

But what disaster—earthquake, explosion, flood, volcano of flame and mud, what lake of fire—had struck and changed the towns of East Texas? What had so crazed the people? What had brought these thousands into towns where they were knotting together and bursting apart like swarming bees? What was their cry? What were they tearing at the earth for? What was the smell in the air, this machinery, this sound of pounding iron? "Oil, podnah," a man told him. "Where you been?"

Was it the coming of the end of the world as prophesied, when flames would rise out of the ground and men would corrupt the face of the earth and turn brother against brother for money and power, and the poor would be corrupted by money and sell their farms and ruin their crops of cotton and cane and corn, turning them into sloughs of mud and burning gas; and country women would wear lipstick and the daughters of the little towns would walk out of the towns on high

heels and go into the oilfields and whore in the toolhouses
and under the reservoirs, fornicating bold as sheep right in
the oilfields, lying in the ditches of the oil reservoirs, spread-
ing to the roughnecks for oil money?

Had he said these things suddenly being given tongue?
Whose words were these? Did he speak them or hear them
disturbing the boom times, shaking the times of plenty, railing
out like John the Baptist? Many said that he was the Second
Coming, the Messiah walking through the exploding fields.
Others said he was a secret agent, a spy, a tool of the big companies trying to get control of the fields from the independent operators. But some of the big oil companies were after
him and sent men out to try to waylay him and beat him up
and run him out of town. They got nowhere, for fear of the
rattlesnake. They had no success except to push Addis and
Jake down into the mud with a pole.

They were ridiculed. Roughnecks wagged their sex at them
and called out foul words. Snake jokes were everywhere.
Whores from cheap cabarets in Mexico yelled to Addis that
they performed a Snake Act he wasn't equipped for. "With
the rattler. Rrrrrr," one added. "Ssssss, honey. Forked tongue,"
another said, darting a lewd member from her large mouth.
The two pilgrims, Addis and Jake, were stoned, hosed with
streams of crude oil. Addis' face was black. The whites of his
huge eyes glowered upon his persecutors, and some were
afraid and some fell down in amazement at his mysterious
look. Was he of another world? Men came after Jake with
clubs and shotguns, shouting, "Kill the snake!" But Addis kept
him close upon his breast and fled in the darkness. He sat on
the edge of a town at night, aching and bleeding, seeing the
fires of the burning oilwells in the distance, and the taste of
oil was bitter in his mouth and the fumes of gasoline scalded
his nostrils. He wept, and had no home.

But the two of them went on through Texas together, Addis
mute and mysterious and enigmatic on the wire, Jake dozing
serenely upon his breast. What was he? What did he mean?

They went on through the mudlands and saltlands and burning holes of the oil lands. Sometimes they were joined and followed for a while by those whose lives had been unbalanced by oil and who vowed for a time—a night, a day, a few hours—to renounce overpowering riches and follow what seemed to be something simply new and unheard of, fleeting, but something of unanswerable and drawing beauty, it could have been no more than the colored flash of a butterfly or a bird or a darting fish—a glimmer, a twinkle, a vision—nothing you could do anything with: a woman broken away from something grand, in a pearl ballgown said to have pure pearls sewn over it, barefooted and befouled with oil, drinking from a quart of Bourbon and falling into the mud; a young man driving a Packard touring car, dressed in a rumpled tuxedo which he said he had been wearing for three days and nights at an orgy and was screwed out of his mind.

Others, mostly the poor in times of affluence, joined the group around Addis as though they had moved to a new town with only a few possessions and bore the air of arriving settlers: dispossessed old people cheated of their land, young rawboned parents with half a dozen dirty children; or other kinds of wanderers: sullen, and dazed, raped girls; lost children who had fled explosions in the night; repentant or bored prostitutes—one, lying in a wagon, with a crated goat and a coop of chickens, said she had made no decision about anything, she was just resting. There was an odd peacefulness and quietness over the curious mobile community—why, nobody knew. Moving by day and settling by night, they formed a sort of outlaw town. Since the towns of Rose County were as disabled as if tornadoes had torn them up and had no peace, the only towns that held together were these odd moving ones. Were they escaping a Gulf hurricane? An advancing enemy? A dust storm? A plague of grasshoppers? And who was this figure, leading such a flock through the flaming orange nights and over the dark, moonless wastes? A revolu-

tionary? A fanatic? A messenger of the Devil? Or just a silent
boy named Addis Adair with a rattlesnake around his neck.

Magical events occurred. At Raccoon Bend a fantastic
young man named Firedevil Prescott went into the holocaust
of a well that had caught fire and put it out like a miracle. In
another town a gusher came in where a man was working and
rose solid into the air like a black pillar with the man sitting
on top of it as if he were a statue. And in another town a
blade of gas like a sword thrust up from the ground and
sliced a shotgun house in two. Debris flew through the air as
furious as shrapnel and fell over Addis and Jake. Was it a war,
was it the end of the world? Yet these two figures, redemp-
tive and prophetic, moved through the stricken Texas towns
astonishing and provoking them. And hearing of the boy on
the wire with the white rattlesnake, those who were afflicted
now sought him. When they came upon him, dragging themselves, or sprawled on cots or riding the backs of others, they
were amazed by the figure in the Switchman's cap who never
said a word, floating upon the wire with a beautiful ruby-
spangled serpent upon his shoulder.

Now, moving behind Addis, like a flight, an exodus, a mi-
gration, there was a caravan of wagons and horses and old
slow used cars, Willys Knights and Ford roadsters and Chev-
rolet coupés pulling homemade trailers loaded with bedding,
a cookstove, children, chickens and ducks. A procession strag-
gled along on foot—moving in solemnity as if led by the hand
of Providence, of Destiny, of God toward a promised land?
—carrying a few possessions, like refugees in a war-torn country. Were they the Chosen People, Gypsies, migrants, a holy
army of the poor, the displaced? Had a great tidal wave rolled
out of the deeps of the land and ruined their cotton lands and
farmland and green gardens, fouled their silage and choked
their animals to death? Were they fleeing poisonous gases that
had broken loose from boiling underground wells and had
suffocated their cows and asphyxiated their blessed mule
teams? What did they have to say if spoken to? What was their

message, their meaning, their hope? No one in the history of Rose County had ever seen or heard reported or read in the Courthouse documents such an unusual phenomenon. Where were they going? Wherever Addis Adair was going, they did not care.

It was surprising how many joined. Sometimes a whole field was full of them, and they moved like a flock through the grasses. Sometimes half a hill and the top of it was covered with them settled there like a flight that had lit there. This floating band of nomads and exiles and outcasts was becoming notorious. It was feared, too. It gathered power. Did it stand for something? Oppose something? Were they pilgrims? Now the bored, restless young (there was a group of adolescents and youths that numbered around fifteen or twenty) joined up. Some of them carried snakes wound around their arms or coiled around their waists. And some carried coils of wire, hoping to imitate Addis.

They gathered under groves of trees when night came, or rested by rivers, in the bottomlands, in dry washes when it had cooled. They pitched tents and made camp. They slept on the ground or in trees. They sang and provided for each other.

It must be admitted that Oil King needed a Number Two. For some months now, while Number One pumped richly on and showed no signs of weakening, none of Oil King's other hunches had materialized. His lessors were getting restless, and a few had become openly suspicious of the independent oil man. People were losing faith in the very man who had taught them faith in the early days. Frankly, Oil King needed something of a miracle. Even his company showed signs of weariness and needed a fresh success. Arab was close to being fed up and Lydia told Oil King that she was getting tired of

hustling money out of mullets—the Oilfield term for investors.
Only Hester and Esther Lane, who seemed never to weary of
playing "Welcome Sweet Springtime," remained unchanged.
They were their same sweet, cheerful selves.

On the Fourth of July, Oil King threw a gala as an all-day
celebration at Number One. This was a more or less desper-
ate attempt to revive flagging excitement. By noon, excitement was still flagging and Oil King was down-at-heart and
pretty blue. Toward midafternoon, in the blazing heat, Oil
King did not see down the distant road what could have been,
in the heat wave, a mirage of (a) the Heavenly Host come to
relieve him of a life of unrelenting anxiety and abuse from his
fellow man or (b) a posse of the law or of citizens taking the
law in their own hands and ambushing him; but he had the
very odd visual sensation of beholding the hallowed figure of
a young man in a cap, holding a cage in his hand and walking
before a large assortment of people in cars, wagons, on horseback and afoot. This could be some wandering biblical tribe,
some scattering of holy people out of captivity, some Exodus,
something of the Old Testament, except for the autos. In his
recent sadness, in his heartsickness that had befallen him since
his business had begun to smell of failure, he thought he had
been seeing things, having dreams and visions of old Bible
things.

Closer on, Oil King saw that the young man was who he
had thought it was, the mute blue boy who that day—a long
time ago, it seemed to him—had walked away down the aisle
of the Revival tent with Jake in his cage, bought for a ten-
dollar bill—a sad red-letter day for Oil King. Now, sure
enough, there in the hands of the boy coming down the road
was the cage of Jake. Overjoyed at the prospect of reunion
with his old friend the white rattlesnake, and wondering who
the crowd was that now followed the boy as once a mob of
adorers had followed him—O sweet days now gone by and
lost!—Oil King ran with open arms to meet Addis Adair and

Jake, as if they were his saviors come to rescue him from despondency and increasing bad news.

Oil King ran to Addis Adair and Jake with more than one special emotion in his breast. High-ranking in the order of feelings in his heart was that of being scared that he might be run out of town by doubters unless a change came about pretty soon. Oil King's old followers of him as Cleon Peters—now investors in his drilling operations—who had followed him at the crossroads the day he got the O.K. message from the Lord to go ahead in his new calling, plus those who'd later joined his enterprise, were seriously close to souring on him and on the verge of being ready for an uprising to get their land or money back. The shows and harangues at Number One were petering out. The people were beginning to fail to see the attraction of the McCrackens getting richer by the minute while the return on their own investments was zero, and Oil King could take the Xylophone and shove it up Arab's ass, as one indignant person suggested. They wanted fresh oil, their *own* oil on *their* land. In such times many a man waited for another man to fall, and one of them was named Wylie Prescott, who was primed to take advantage of this incendiary situation and turn it to his own benefit as the most promising young wildcatter waiting in the wings to emerge when the right moment came. In this world of quick fortunes one man went down and another rose up before you could tell what had happened.

"People been voicing their unhappiness with the failure of oil to make an appearance on their property," Arab had informed Oil King. "To 'manifest itself'—to use your words—which, I'm beginning to believe, is a lot of shit."

"Now, now, Long Boy, don't fall back!" Oil King said. "Don't fall prey to doubts and, especially, your old foul sinful lan-

guage that you was using in profusion—every other word was
fuckin—when I pulled you like a molar tooth outa your seat
and up my aisle that night in Toluca, Texas; saved your soul
and changed your life."

"You through?" asked Arab. He waited a moment. "Add to
what I've just told you, may I continue, people bitching because nobody showed up to test for oil at their place after
they paid their fu . . . paid their money."

"People never satisfied. What'd they expect for ten dollars?"

"Oil," advised Arab.

"Hell, I caint put oil *in* the ground," Oil King answered.

"Think about that," said Arab.

"The Lord put it in, Oil King takes it out. You know that."

"Lord's only one here puttin it in," growled Arab, "and nobody's takin anything out, as far as I can tell."

"You gettin downhearted, old friend?"

"I'm not so much downhearted as I'm smelling instead of
oil—hot tar. And chickenfeathers."

"Well, everbody got to have them some patience. I caint
get around to everbody over night. Only got two knees. And
they got callouses from kneeing my way over half this territory. Livin my life dog-fashion, if you get right down to it."

"Well, if you get right down to it, lots of them are getting
tired of waiting, just like they did before, when you had em
all toeing the line and ready to run for the gates to Heaven
when the end-of-the-world trumpet blasted. Humans get tired
of waiting, Oil King. They need signs. And they need them
some *results*. *Material* results." In trying to reason with his
master, Arab seemed to be talking about himself as well, seeing that he was working on a commission.

"Wasn't like this when we was doin Christian work," Arab
whined.

Oil King let himself fall into a sudden revery. "Blessed ole
Jake. Sure need him now."

"You need *somethin*, or you ain't goin to have fuckin *nothin*."
Arab scowled. "*Atall*."

Suddenly it was apparent to Oil King how mean and low Arab really could get if he had to. But just when he had been feeling so blue and rebuked, what he had seen was no dream but the boy bringing Jake to him, as if wishing for him had made it come true.

On the little platform by the side of Number One where Oil King's show was performed, stood Addis Adair holding the cage with Jake in it. There was such a throng surrounding the stage, such a mass gathering made up of the mixture of Oil King's people and Addis Adair's followers, that no one could remember any spectacle that had ever brought so many together in one place—no circus or Chautauqua or Revival—nor such a variety and mixture of ages and sizes and human conditions. As far, almost, as the eye could see, there was a field filled with people as soundless as the ghosts of the dead, as rapt and as austere as the shades of the dead called up before Judgment. It seemed that time and all the world had hushed and stopped. It could have been a great multitude of people witnessing an event of history, of the saints such as was painted on the domes of early churches. Was it Pentecost, was it Doomsday? Then there was a sound and was it a bed creaking, a rusty door cracking open? And what was the soft gushing sound, the stifled drumbeat rhythmic and steady? It was Number One suddenly audible; had it, too, stood still for a time?

Against the voluptuous squash of Number One and over the countless heads of the immobile multitude, Oil King hurled like a splash of water a cry: "Brothers and Sisters! Lord God A-mighty!"

The crowd was brought to life and something mysterious circulated through it, something temporarily dead but now revived, causing a low hum and whisper to rise dimly up from within it, as if it were one body. This was the biggest congregation ex-Cleon Peters had ever in his life had or dreamed of. He was going to give the sermon of his life, the Show for which destiny had molded him.

"The holy serpent! Old Jake's cage!" He moved toward the cage with hands outstretched, and it seemed that he might be going to take up Jake in his own hands again. This astonished the crowd and clenched them tighter together, as if it had made them breathless. Oil King had them in his grasp again.

"I know a lot of you fainthearted ones won't believe me when I state that tears still well up in my eyes and a throb beats in this old heart of mine to see this cage and remember them old days when I was carrying it around. You all remember them too! The days when you had faith. I don't know who you new people are this boy brought here, but I say to you, *Join up with me.* Come in to my wildcat operations! Faith without works is dead!" Now the crowd was certain that Oil King was moving to open the cage and take the snake to his breast as he had done in the old days.

But Oil King did not open the cage. He cried out in mock drama, acting as if the serpent had struck him in his breast. He wailed, "I feel his sting, running all through me, up and down and around through my body. I'm shudderin with his sting, and I'm steeling myself against his purple poisonin running through my veins, but I will not fall! I'll keep my faith! He will not strike me down!"

Oil King had got so divided and it was so clear that he had lost a lot of his old faith that, if he had picked up Jake, Jake would have been equally confounded and therefore not sure where he himself stood or where faith lay. Under these clouded conditions the snake might have struck Oil King; and Oil King, separated within himself, weakened at his center, might have died from Jake's poison. However, what you'd think would have happened did *not* occur—that is, Jake did not get a chance even to check the state of his faith, much less to bite Oil King and kill him. Besides, Oil King had more sense than to impair his life at such a time as this. Add to this that, before much of anything could happen, a horrible event took place.

Some men, servants of Wylie Prescott, ran up on the platform and seized Oil King and right before the eyes of everybody—and with Number One pumping heartily away—stripped his clothes off him and tarred and feathered him in full view of the horrified crowd which fell into panic. The men called, "Swindler!" and the crowd broke apart as if it had burst asunder and the lame were shambling and the dumb were howling in terror and the hale were mixed with the halt. Oil King's crowd mixed in with Addis Adair's as if they had been sifted together. They might have formed a kind of army and advanced upon the tarrers and featherers had not three men held loaded shotguns against them.

But arms were not necessary. The smell of tar-cooked flesh, the odor of burnt chicken and duck feathers were enough to turn people away—worse than tear gas—from poor howling Oil King.

"Blue Boy with the snake, holy saint of the road, save me from this humiliation and pain! Faithful Jake! Turn the curse of the ages upon this generation of vipers that so persecutes me!"

And was Oil King going to deliver a sermon in his old style, rolling out of his throat of the old days, as if he had a tape deck in there? No, for he could not shout over the tumult before him, the collision of wagons and autos, the whinnying of horses and the shrieks of humans. Was this pandemonium before him the Day of Judgment he had so often visualized as he preached the end of the world? Had Addis brought the end of the world upon him—was *he*, oh my God, the Second Coming? Who would have thought that it would end like this, him, Rev. Cleon Peters, befeathered and stalking on chicken legs like some big evil fowl of Satan and not rising winged in light, beatific and angelic as he had dreamt. It was Damnation, this Second Coming. Satan had won. Satan was victori-

ous. Hell was the Eternity he had misguessed. What a surprise! There was no Heaven! He had been led into the hands
of thugs by this young Judas-boy; and Jake had been the
abominable Serpent condemned to the dust of the ground and
biting out of the mud at the heels of humanity. Everything was
turned over and corrupted unto Eternity. In this hallucination
of horror and damnation he passed out.

Addis and Jake fled, but the men got Arab and pulled his
pants down and threw him to the floor and shouted, "Pervert!"
and that they were going to do a terrible thing to him, but
evidently decided against it since he was later seen running
bare-naked through the town, intact.

The oilfields were in an uproar. Was it a massacre? A revolution? A great fowlish figure of feathers that seemed to
change into a shape made of boiling black smoke and howling
as if it were human, fled through the bogs and mires of the
oilwastes at twilight, dreadful.

Knowing they were after him and Jake, Addis hid under a
reservoir and huddled over Jake's cage to protect him. Sometime in the dreadful night he opened the cage to comfort Jake,
and it was then that he saw that Jake was not there. Lost!
Where in the hellwash of that violent night was the gentle and
defenseless white rattlesnake? He wept and he lay upon the
cold earth and did not want to live.

All night he could hear the shouts and curses of the men
sent by the powerful Wylie Prescott to catch Addis and Jake.
"Snake Freak!" they called.

How they despised a low-bellied snake. They'd tarred the
old snake-handling fourflusher; now they'd get the snake and
the boy. Fuckin snake. If you see a snake, kill 'im; and if you
find a radical damned Communist of the unions, like the boy

causing labor riots and unrest in the oilfields, catch him and take care of him. That was what Wylie Prescott's men thought.

Their boss, Wylie Prescott, was coming up fast now. Within twenty-four hours after the routing of Oil King, he had bought out Number One and he had bought up Oil King's leases, cheap, from his disgruntled clients, and had started one of the big oil companies of the oilfields. It was in this way that the poor leases in Oil King's simple possession, held by cheap liens of five and ten dollars, and most of which, lying drenched in oil, he had not had time to get around to, turned out to be the most fabulous oilfield in East Texas—the Prescott Field of Rose County. But more of this directly, for lonesome and hunted Addis is still on our mind.

Early in the morning before sunrise it became quiet, his pursuers had gone in another direction, and then was when Addis put a heavy stone in Jake's cage and sank it in a water-well on a ruined farm. Then Addis began his last journey, bereaved and without home or companion. He doubled back toward where he started, having made this curve like the flight of an insect. He had moved, it seemed—and was probably true—a thousand miles, over half Texas, an unexplainable flight that had taken the shape of a half-circle. As he returned he went by night past his old town of Rose, walking the railroad tracks past Jewel's house that seemed unreal now and a place of which he had only a dim memory, like a piece of a dream remembered. He went on, toward the ruined Round-house.

Ace's tomb in the ruins was no longer troubled. Now it was a green mound mossy with fern and garlanded with blooming Trumpet and Morning-glory and Honeysuckle vines. In this moist place teeming with blooms unsucked and heavy, hanging untouched fruits oozing musk in the humid early morning twilight, Addis saw that Ace's place of violent death had been overtaken by another kind of passion: and now what he felt was not sorrow for the loss of Ace, not grief, but such an overwhelming vitality, such a surge and rush of male power that he could use it to procreate a generation, to populate a town. If he clasped a fruit, cleft open by fullness or stretched by ripeness, it burst out warm juice. If he touched the opening of a blossom it gave way, warm and sliding, to his press and it seemed to softly clutch and draw his fingertip. There were arching stems that could barely support heavy-crested heads of buds which, when he held them on his palm, seemed fleshly. What was this fruit of such softness and warmth, human in its heat and softness, that hung so tight and heavy and full? He eased its load—a kind of milk flushed out. Surely there was a resurrection out of this once accursed place, a resurrection of Ace's soul—Addis knew this already; but now he felt the passionate redemption of Ace's flesh. The vitality of Ace, revived and empowered, went into Addis.

Suddenly a man, virile and ripe, he turned and went on away toward the hidden wilderness, and by clear dawn he had vanished into the Big Thicket.

10

The Green Tree
and The Dry

The Thicket was knitted, locked and hooked onto itself, into a huge knotted textile of tree and vine, a woven artifice worked under another hand, a fortress nature had constructed against civilization of towns and systems made by men's hands. The Thicket was a vault of iron man could not unlock and open. It was like a vast quicksand that would close over and suffocate anyone who got in it—a trap, a citadel, a walled society, a commune of wildness, of beast and serpent and fowl. It bloomed and mated, devoured and salvaged itself, without the intercession of mankind. With its life in its own possession, it would go on forever.

In a little opening of the locked undergrowth, where there was a clear piece of ground near a majestic tree which spread a shelter and entangled its branches with other trees, Addis Adair built a hut out of the very stuff of the Thicket— twigs as strong as beams, leaves as thick as shingles and mortared with mud—and there he lived. He locked himself in the woods in the bramble that was a spiked barricade, as if he were behind bars and barbed wire. He enclosed and imprisoned himself behind the fence of ironlike wire and cablelike root and branch. Except for the few winter months when

there was a gentle frost and sometimes delicate ice, the
weather of the Thicket was soft and warm. In the summer it
was very hot, but the deep-green shade made it cool. In the
pale-yellow sunlight that fell through the great canopy of
leaves over him, he made a kind of garden in the clearing
around his little dwelling. Life was a chain of nights and days,
sun and moon, big stars, the song of birds, the grunts and cries
of animals. He never spoke a word. In his hut he lay and felt
the secret sexual movement of the Thicket. Who could touch
it? It was so clenched upon itself, growing in and out of itself, self-seeding, self-incubating, self-mothering, that it was
a woven construction of vine, like its veins, and sap, its
blood. It spurted out itself, its own stuff, its self-continuation.
It throbbed and pulsed like a gonad in the groin of Texas,
so ripe and enjuiced with life. Its power was in its magical
chain, passing itself on from itself to itself in abundance,
self-enriched, self-continued. Who harmed this precious link-
age, fouled life. The blessing of the colored birds, the gentle,
building animals of nests, lair, dam, the carnal violence, the
musical, secret life of the Thicket entered his very soul. He
ate what he found, killed nothing, built no fire, made scarcely
a sound. The animals lived around him and Ace in their kind
of garden of paradise. Once the murderous sound of an ax
against a tree, the thudding sound of deathblow struck his
body as if it were the very tree. And for more nights there
appeared the spectral orange looming of a fire far off, lowering
and pulsing and quivering. He and the animals knew a disaster was happening, and they lay low in a kind of hushed
prayer. Another time some kind of machine was whirring like
an ungodly beast way off somewhere. And once in a while
the roar of a rushing train engine trembled the Thicket, or
the steaming thunder of a gushing oilwell, and he saw the
hellish fire-shadow and smelled the faint sour odor of burning oil.

It was a wondrous ancient tree, gigantic around its trunk, which was like the skin of something of the old earth, natal and maternal and sexual and tall and broad as a building, of an extraordinary shape. It held in its crown, upraised, a lyre-shaped arrangement of branches. The two upward-curving branches were in a praising shape, an embracing shape.

When Addis strung his wire between the two upraised branches, it looked like a lyre of one string. Over this lyre of branches arched a tent of dense leaves and interlacing vines. This tree in the wilderness of the Thicket was something which Mr. de Persia might have constructed, it was so efficient and exquisite. But nature, not an artificer, had made this tree, and this magnificent creation had sustained itself and endured in wildness. Where the wire was strung between the two upreaching branches was a green and shadowy bower in the very heart of the tree, under a very delicate shelter, a magical place. This was the boy's theater. The wire was stretched between the two branches in the same way a piece of string could be stretched between two fingers, between the thumb and the great finger.

At night, when the moon was full and bright, a figure would come like a night bird, a moth, and ascend as nimbly as a tree animal, the giant live oak. When he reached the open bowl, he took from his shoulder a coil of silver in the moonlight, a clothesline. And then, like a spider at work in the moonlight, he strung the wire across the bower, from branch to branch.

Naked he walked across the wire, precariously balancing himself, teetering and winging the air with his arms to keep himself aloft and in balance. The flamboyant and fearless performer in the top of the tree was in his bower, his theater, his garden, his voluptuous bower, his seminal garden, his theater of generation.

He had begun lower down in the tree, in small openings of branches, over short distances. As he became surer of himself he moved up, higher and higher, climbing, at his own rate and according to his increasing magical prowess, the tree, until he was finally in the very crown of the tree in heights that seemed empyreal, celestial, of the sky and clouds and stars, a height beyond measurement—*aloft*. In the lower region of the tree Addis had worn his old starry cowboy boots and his frayed satin top hat, but when he had reached the topmost heights, he walked naked, totally in nature and a part of the tree, balancing himself with a large palmetto leaf. Now in the breathtaking ascents of the very tower of the great live oak he was able to perform fantastic feats on the wire. He had become transfigured in the tree, enchanted creature of the Thicket, bewitched figure of the live oak. He leapt, tripped, froze and made a dazzling statue on the wire; he perched on one foot; he breathlessly pirouetted slowly like a mechanical figure: a figure on a clock, on a bell tower, on a music box. He hopped, a bird. He fluttered, a moth. Utterly naked on the wire in the blue wilderness moonlight or in the green wilderness sunlight, he felt melted into the whole world of sky and woods, vines, flowers, grass. He was engulfed by the wild sensual moonlight, naked with the white moths shimmering around him, in the very bosom of the tree.

In this wonderful tree on whose brotherly trunk he had hung the tobacco can with Ace's photo in it, Addis Adair, marvelous ornament, walked naked on the clothesline he had stolen from Jewel's house—oh so long ago, it seemed to him now. His erect penis, bowed like a Satyr's, guided him like a compass needle, balancing him, weighting him and buoying him aloft, leading his steps like a wand, a baton, keeping him afloat, child of air and eroticism, like a life preserver. Often as he moved on the wire in his voluptuous bower, his seminal garden, he shot his seed into the air, silver-white and flashing in the moonlight. Shooting! The flushing pulses and charges of shining white and silver burst from him and flung through the moonlit air, some unearthly creature of wilderness that had lighted there, coming out of the mysterious drumming deeps of the forest where tree linked with tree, locked as if by handclasps. His body played upon the tree like a harp and the tree seemed to tremble around him as though he, moving and throbbing through it, *in* it, working, struggling in it, were loving it, fucking the tree; and the tree dazzled and trembled through the body of this beautiful flirting and flickering and shooting figure, phantom and elusive and mystical, in its innocent heat, its virgin holiness, its wilderness glory.

The day Jewel Adair came upon it was like a vision. There in the distance, in that green cave in the heart of the great tree, a figure hovered with arms spread out like wings. It seemed to hang in air. She watched, almost without breathing, and she saw that the figure was a boy and that it was poised on a wire strung between two branches. It was as if something had spun this figure in the tree, out of a web or a cocoon. It was such a tree thing, so delicate and swinging and airy.

Suddenly, silently, the delicate and graceful figure glided over the wire in the tree. A figure walking in the top of a tree! In the top of the tree in the serenity of his bower, a boy floated across a wire. Birds, orange and scarlet and blue, flashed around him in the green light. But he might fall! She gasped. And then she saw that beneath the tree on the ground was a soft and humid cushion of leaves, petals, fruits, seeds, mull, twigs, feathers and fur that lay beneath him to catch him like a net.

She lay in the bushes behind a screen of leaves and

watched, hardly breathing. He hung like something of the tree itself, an acorn, a cone, the very seed of the tree.

And she thought she heard a flirting measure of music, fluttering in the dark, nearing the dim moment where it might be recognized, almost there, then receding into the dark, vanishing then, faintly toning its haunting melody. She wanted, to the quick of her fingernails, the nipples of her breasts and in the depth of her womb, the boy in the tree. But what's more: her very soul, the very soul of Jewel Adair entered the figure before her.

She fled, but at home she was haunted by the figure in the tree. She found no rest; everywhere she saw the shape of the visionary figure. The image of the wirewalker in the tree was burned upon her sight.

She came back, watching him from a distance at first. She crept closer and closer. Where did he come from? Where did he live? Once he almost fell, and she gasped so loud that she feared he might hear her. She was that close!

And then she realized that she had been in the Thicket for a long space of time, how many days or nights she did not know. She was impassioned beyond reality now, enraptured beyond her senses. She became quite crazed. In the dark, humid underbrush she hid, naked, and panted and throbbed, drenched with her heats. She lay spread and opened in the warm leaves and moaned voluptuously in her hot agony and yearning and hunger. She tore at herself. Her rich breasts had become engorged with longing and their nipples were red and ripe and big as strawberries; and her sex burned and ached and was now so full-lipped and swollen between her thighs, so strutted and puffed with itching desire, that to walk excited her to near-madness.

She was possessed by this tree god, this treedevil, this boy who was the bloom of the tree, gorgeous and infernal, holy, divine, evil, profane. Jewel Adair was now bound by the wirewalker's spell cast over her, enchanted and accursed. Who would come to save her, break the hellish spell over her, bring her ease and mercy and relief from this torment, this longing for the boy in the tree that was like dying?

One day Addis saw from the wire in the top of the tree a naked woman standing in the clearing. He gasped and almost fell at the blinding sight of the voluptuous body. He had never seen a naked woman. In his fantasies he had imagined what one would look like, and he had talked to the photo of Ace about it (poor Ace, hearing about what he, himself, had scarcely seen!), told him of his wondering and his yearning and his need for the naked body of a woman. Now here it was—or was he having a vision out of his solitude and endless lonesomeness. But no—she turned and looked upwards. And was she beckoning? Was that look in her calling him, beckoning him down from his heights? He trembled and walked to the tree and held on to it. Now she moved behind a palmetto, and the sight of her belly and luxuriant pubic hair through the hairy fronds of the palmetto enfevered him and made him feel giddy and faint in the tree. And her breasts! To gather them and rub his naked body against them! Now she moved through the grass of the clearing and passed languid and sensual through the blooming vines into a little hidden shelter under a low leafy branch of the live oak, looking up at him as he stood naked in the tree beckoning—yes she was calling him down to her.

He was against her, as though he had flown down. He held her naked body against his naked body and buried his head in her breasts. And what was it that took him over and moved him against her and thrust him into her—he was into her body! It was her hand that seized him where no hand but his own had ever been, and it was her hand that slipped him into the heat of her as if he had sliced her hot flesh. She pulled him down onto the soft mattress of sweet-smelling

leaves and fallen blooms and she drew him into her and
fucked him deeply, truly, utterly. She used him until she was
exhausted. And then, gasping, she whispered, "Again! again!
I want it again! Fuck me!" What was this fury clinging to him,
of bristle and velvet, this pounding bone and flesh, this unbearable suction that drew up his very breath and life out of
him? A whirlwind of the softest winds had seized him, a
whirlpool of velvet slickness was twisting him, something hot
and wet and slippery and meaty was sliding in and out of
him and he was not being able to stand it and yet bearing it
and then not being able to endure it again, on and on;
something poured upon him, from him. He saw her hair matted
with leaves and caked with earth, her face like a wild
woman's, and she ground her teeth and flinched her thighs
and squeezed her eyes with pain. It seemed endless. Each
time she reached the peak of her lust and it broke upon her,
she jerked away in starts and leaps and then fell back and
thrashed her head as if she were being hit, as if she had received a blow. She rode him like a furious mare, tossing her
long hair, head thrown back and snorting. He was beyond
himself, as if he had been caught by something rushing and
was being dragged on with it. He was blinded and dumbfounded by her raging, voluptuous hunger. He stayed with
her, clinging to a bucking, heaving animal in the throes of
some cursed endlessness.

When she was finally spent and could no longer move, she
rested, breathing like a dying creature. And finally she looked
at him, pressed against her beaten flesh, and murmured, "Who
are you, who are you? You'll kill me." He only closed his eyes
and felt as if he were dying.

The heat and slipperiness, the almost unbearable slipping
of her flesh over his flesh was an ecstasy to him; but what
really astonished him was her immense want, her unappeasable gluttony for him, her starvation. She seemed truly possessed of him, she seemed crushed by her lust for him. It was
almost self-destroying in its voracity. She came almost to

humiliate herself upon him. She began to degrade herself with his body, on and on—where was she? What body was this? It seemed to have no head, but yes, there it was, between his legs—and oh her mouth, her tongue! and now where had she gone, leaving only a tight, hurting muscle of slime seizing him like a trap. And then they slept. When she woke he was gone.

Then she would see him again, there in the top of his tree, standing on the wire, looking down at her. She moved through the bush to the tree and sat under the low branch, on their now blessed mattress of grass, waiting. Soon she would hear the cracking and waterfall sound of his descent to her through the leaves. He came down naked and stood before her. She pulled him down to her and did not even wait but pulled him inbetween her legs into her. And then she tore at his sex within her and writhed until she fainted away in a wild whooping sound which startled him and seemed like an animal of the deep Thicket wilderness, there where they were, hidden in their tree-shadowed and tree-covered bower. But now, as she took a breath, she had so aroused him with her heat and soft gamey richness that he plunged against her and threw her over and thrust into her and worked upon her in a passion beyond his senses, in an uncontrollable fucking. A new thing started: he became like her. Thus they went, touch-and-go, one taking the other's thrust, seesaw, a human machine, a wheel-driven machine of some kind, a pump, a dynamo, in the deep Thicket, in the hidden bower, under the marvelous tree. Animals watched them. Their cries rang through the jungle forest like any other creatures'.

After she would leave, he'd lie under the tree in a curious half-sleep; or many nights he'd lie awake in his hut, haunted, exhausted but wanting her even then. Where had she gone? She had moved away like a ghost into the darkness. Was she a dream, a spell, a madness that had come over him? He felt he might go mad if he couldn't have her *now*. Fantasies, visions of her tormented him. He was possessed of her. Lubri-

cious images of her besieged him; the bloom on her, and the
sweetness, and the broad, wide, plump, tight hairiness of her.
Her depth and softness clutching him! He was blinded by
such realistic images of her sex, the very fold and wink and
cut of it, that he thought he could reach and touch it: her sex
sucked and pouted before his eyes, hung hairy and swollen
and wet and open; or it rose from under her big belly, wide
and broad, a firm, split swelling as big as his hand, that
could scarcely cover it, cupping it and grasping it like a warm
grisly living thing, rolling it and molding it and piercing it and
handling it, all of it, all split open like a big tight melon, as it
quivered and sucked, oral and swallowing, or grabbed his
fingers and seemed to struggle with his hand, this big, live
hot meaty being that lay in there, humid and grainy and
viscous and hairy, between her legs and slit up her soft shaggy
belly. He was blinded by her devouring cunt. He would fall
to the ground and cry out, beating the ground with his fists.
Where was his lonesomeness, where was his sweet pure orphanage? He cursed the woman and struck out blindly at
her damned and damning sex before him, but he was blinded
by it, it now seemed like the very lashes on his eyes. His tree,
his hut became a prison, a hell. He tore at himself and did
nothing but wait for her. If she did not come, he would
pull at himself and tear at his raw swollen sex and shoot off
upon the tree trunk or on their mattress of leaves and grass.
"Ace!" he cried. "Save me from this death!" If he thought he
heard her footfall, he would run. Once when he found it was
a deer, he clubbed it in a savage rage until it fought for its
life and ran off half-slaughtered.

But nothing could save him from her. The absence of her
belly, of the whole hairy, wet slit of her, of the very hole of
her, tight and clinching, of the slick throbbing, almost chewing tube of her, this absence was the absence of all reality,
the absence of the world. The memory of her hunching on
him, her crotch wide open and laid out upon his crotch, rasp-
ing and swabbing and mashing his genitals, the lapping

sounds as he slipped in and out, until she pressed so heavily upon him that some part of her, way deep and up in her, seized the head of him and drew his sperm out of him in such hurting ecstasy that he growled and grunted and howled, there in the wild Thicket. Something burst in his brain and seemed to break open his whole body, spurting from his very core everywhere in what felt like rage in him, an angry fury, something of pain and sweetness, wild and furious with sweet pain running up and down the length of him.

She did not come. The sensations obsessed him, lingering in his flesh, and he would dream back through the sense of fucking Jewel; driving it, it had become so hard and thick he could just barely move it in her; his buttocks had control of it like a lever, like a club, like a crane; his buttocks manipulated it like a strong pole. And shooting! Shooting on the wire had been all he had known. This was new, shooting through the hard length of it, encased and contained and held tight; that feeling! Flushing pulses; hot spurting; feeling the stuff break and burst through the mouth of it into the air, so strong it lashed his cock; his cock was only a channel for it, the come, the come was the thing; coming through it lashed and shook it, tore, burning, through it, hurtling out and through—and out and away from him; thrown out from him, cast, shot. Sometimes he felt as if he had shot his whole cock into her, like a thick arrow from his very body, which was a bow. Or that his whole cock exploded and shattered inside her, like a grenade. Then he felt he had literally given his cock to her, that he was cockless. She had taken it, the whole thing had gone off in her, into her: his thighs and buttocks, his groin had hunched and hurled it into her, like a grenade. He could not stop thinking of it. And oh had Ace shared this with him, Ace who witnessed it from his photo in the tobacco can on the tree, Ace whose presence had been all around him, had Ace hunched with him and come, at last, at long last, with him in his near-madness of lust. Yes, he knew that Ace was there, with him in his sexual heat and his cruel lust and in his bestial convulsion. In the new mystery of his sex, Ace was there; in the revolution, the fire and the shattering and the newness of the world, Ace was there; and in the sadness of manhood, the sadness of come, the sorrows of woman-lust, the sorrows of comers, the frailty of coming manhood, in that old male-sorrow, father-sorrow . . . there was Ace; he was there!

And still Jewel did not come. The ravens came, filling his days with their human-sounding voices and grieflike calls. A gigantic quivering flight of infernal white moths came in silently and settled like cotton in the green growth and devoured whole trees, and his nights twinkled with deadly moths; they clung to the wire as if to try to devour metal and they covered the tree like lace. He tried to walk his wire. Now, in the blue moonlight he was naked but wearing the moths like a white fleece; his whole body was trembling with the moths, and his white sperm flew from him like moths again and, cruelly coming as though it was his whitened blood tossed from him in the tree, he went blind with fury and madness and heartbreak, in despair and bitter ecstasy, wailing the cry of the lost.

Who came and saw this swaying woman under a live oak tree cradling a naked figure in her lap? This woman nursing manhood, nursing him as the tree had nursed him, swaying him in her bosom as the tree had swayed with him at its breast—mother, woman, nurse—who came and saw her? She had lowered Addis from the low-hanging branch of the tree to her shoulders, carried him upright on her back until he fell back down the length of her as though he were grabbing at her ankles.

She had found him where he hung by his jaws from the crotch of two plump branches of the tree. Like a diver chuting feet-first into a glistening green water of light and leaves, he had dropped through a harnesslike arrangement of branches and by violent force thrust down to his jawbones, where he was yoked. His blowing lips mouthed the tree cleft; and his balled eyes were squeezed through their sockets as if they were two creatures, porcelain and eyelike, being delivered in birth through two hairy orifices.

He hung like something of the tree itself, the very seed of it. His penis was rigidly arched at a sixty-degree angle to his body in the classical Satyr's bowed cock of lasciviousness. This striking priapic figure hanging in the live oak tree astounded Jewel, and she cried out oh how will I bring down the hanged boy?

She stood between his legs and shouldered him. And then she heaved up her shoulders and lifted him free of his yoke. He fell back and she clasped him to her by his ankles round her breasts, and his full length was flung down her back, his hair tossing to touch the ground. He was some extravagant bloom of the tree. She bore him thus away on her back to their place under the tree, against the great body of the tree. Then she squatted and lowered him gently to the ground; and then she bent forward and slowly, heavily stretched herself out out on the ground, unrolling his body under hers until they lay together; and that was when they made the child, she knew to God; the last life of the boy of the wire in the tree was thrust into her and then he shuddered and shot his last life into her. And then she lifted him into her lap and sat under the great mysterious tree of his death, rocking the hanged boy in the cradle of her arms. And that was when she saw the harp-shaped birthmark on the thigh of Addis Adair.

There's a shallow grave in the Thicket as deep as Jewel Adair could dig it. Birds hop on it; all kinds of little animals of the woods leave their tracks on it. And in the grave lies beautiful Addis Adair, nestled among the great tree roots in a nest of tangled roots. With him in the ground is a frazzled satin top hat, a bouquet of wilderness white hawthorn and a tobacco tin, with a photograph in it. And hanging in the tree is a rusted length of clothesline.

All day she dug a grave under the tree, there under the soft mattress where they had lain. Toward evening she had opened a hole around the cables and chains of roots long and deep enough for him to lie in. There was a nestlike weaving of velvet roots at the depth of the hole, and she laid the dancing boy in this nest, working his arms and legs under and around the roots. He was woven, plaited into the core, the sexual hub, of the tree. When she looked down, she saw that already the tree had grasped him to its dark sexual life as it had flashed him in the sunlight like a leaf of its own. The tree into which he had showered his rich nature as he walked the wire had gathered him now to its darkest place, to its place of power and mystery, to its own sexual fierce engine, to its mysterious works, its deep loins where it worked, like the moiling of testicles, its secret power. Then was when she saw the mark shaped like a harp on his thigh, and oh to my Lord and Savior she knew it was Addis Adair. And then she found the tobacco can with the photo of Ace in it, hanging on the tree.

She fell on her knees and heard, as though she had been struck to the ground by it, the soft voice of Ace. *Didn't you know when we married I would want to do that to you? If it's so wrong, then I swear to God I don't know what to do. Because I just can't put it out of my mind . . . But I'll try to live up to you, Jewel. Just help me and give me time. God has given me a saint for a wife and my temptations have been put on me by the Devil to try to smut up God's own saint. Guess I'd be in the gutter if it wasn't for you. I'd kill myself first, before I'd ugly up something pure and good as you are, swear to God.*

And then in her infernal vision she saw Ace's face in the flame and roar of the exploded switch engine, and she saw him go down in the sunken locomotive.

She went mad. She thought she saw Addis in the tree, falling, and she thought she saw Ace on his knees praying and suffering. She saw Addis hanging with a purple choked face, tongue jammed out of his mouth and his sex hard and huge. And she heard the wail of Ace over the skidding and blast of iron, calling from the locomotive, "Jewel! Jewel! Jew-ell! Jew-ell!"

She threw herself naked on Addis' grave and clawed in the dirt of it, and covered with dirt, ran like a savage woman through the woods, howling.

It was Mr. de Persia who saw this, first on a moonlit night when he heard what he thought was a human sound. He went toward the sound, and when he saw the sight it was of a naked beastlike woman whose hair on her head hung wild and tangled over her face and shoulders and over her enormous breasts, and whose groin hair grew shaggy around her brute sex, which was like another head, and up her belly and down her thighs almost to her knees. Was this some monstrous and forlorn Thicket creature bred there by the mating of some animal and some human? He had heard stories of such creatures. There had been one in a carnival sideshow; it had hooves of a goat and licked out its lascivious tongue. He saw her run on, like a raving spirit, a crazed fury, some haunted figure, howling like a woman in childbirth or in sexual climax. She vanished into the darkness.

The next time Mr. de Persia saw the tormented figure of the woman was on a late shadowy afternoon. She was hanging from the dangling wire in the tree. When he went, afraid, to the great tree, he found a grave under it. It was an unsettled and troubled grave. Its earth had been so churned and

trodden that it must hold an evil spirit, he thought. There
was a crude marker stabbed into the grave, and on it was
scrawled, *Not Mine But Another Man's Son*. What was this
sad story that Mr. de Persia would never know? What had
gone on here that had ended like this? He was standing in
the ruins of something of suffering and passion that would
remain a secret forever. And who was lying in the disturbed
grave? Why had he never seen this place before, or this
woman? But the Thicket was so vast and there were so many
hidden places. He never wandered far from his place,
anyway. He had found a cave half-covered with moss and
lived there during the hidden years of his life that led to
oblivion; whose son? This sight before him made him ask himself what was his meaning, what was the shape of his life?

How would he rescue the swinging body from the tree?
And what was this wire, bound to the tree on one end as it
was bound to the woman's neck on the other end? It swung
sometimes slowly round and round like a caterpillar on its
thread, sometimes pendulumlike while the limb of the tree
clicked like a clock. Ravens sat in the tree. He counted seven,
for a secret never to be told.

Poor soul, God save her, what thing had she done that so
drove her to this? thought Mr. de Persia. And how will I ever
bring her down from the tree? He was old now, and though
he had been a strong, big man, age and the rigors of his life
in the Thicket had weakened him. Once the very figure of
vigor all over the country, the image of rank physical force,
impertinent, arrogant, formidable, he was now a venerable,
quietened old man, somehow purified, purged, cleansed,
released and liberated: a changed being, a new man. Had he
been born in the Thicket, like the animals he lived among?
He had no memory beyond it. It seemed to him that he had
always been there. When he was born—or discovered himself—drenched in natal fluid and in a sodden wet white cloth,
he had found a creek and a spring and shed his covering and
bathed himself in the pure clear cool water. He was born!

And where he was born was a wild garden. He lived in it, day and night, through a chain of peaceful sequences of light and dark. He sat at the mouth of his cave, dozing, or walked through the great deep woods.

All night he was in the tree, struggling to get to the hanged woman by the light of the moon. Tree animals, squirrels and chipmunks—and the seven ravens—watched. The great tree rustled in the sweet night air, as Mr. de Persia struggled in it. His faded robe of parachute cloth billowed like a sail in the tree and encumbered his climbing, and he stopped often to unsnag himself.

He came closer and closer. His view of her was obscene, and she looked like some demon of lewdness such as had tempted and tormented the saints. She was Eve whored. "Oh my Savior!" he whispered. "This woman has died in evil, in lust. She is a figure of damnation and desire."

He slowly ascended through the leaves, resting on a branch or hugging the great trunk or clawing into the bark. He rose, heavy and slow and clambering, through the labyrinth of twigs and leaves. Now he was on a level with her and she suddenly swung toward him, hunching her shaggy pelvis toward him as if to devour him with her great vagina, opened and sexual as if it had been freshly thrust into, and he reached out for her.

It was Oil King who found the spectacle of two hanging shapes in the tree. He was having a vision, something of the Apocalypse, of the book of Revelation, was what he saw—a mystical beast strung high in the tree and a creature that seemed to be suspended in air from a parachute gathered around his neck. Only his head was above it—but there was his large body hanging bare, shucked out of the cloth like an ear of corn, and skinned back by the forked branch through which he had fallen.

And then the signs of the End of the World burst forth and were shewn to him, as he later told, and he knew, in an instant, everything. "Oh Lord, at long last!" he cried, weeping and praising his Savior. "You've come, you've come!" And then controlling himself, as one long trained in preparation for this event, perfectly programed for it, he marched like the ready Christian soldier that he was, without another moment's hesitation, toward the Heavenly Signs, led by what appeared to be a path of light, lamp unto his feet, out of the Thicket.

Part II

THE ERA OF
WYLIE PRESCOTT

11

The Coming of
Firedevil Prescott

When Firedevil Prescott fought the fires of the boomtown oilwells and air was filled with mud and rocks and air was sour-sweet with tarry smell of oil, was special days, not like now, not dreary days of sameness like now. Hull and Saratoga and Daisetta and Raccoon Bend was nothing but mud and oil, slicky and up to your ankles and shiny with oil rainbows— ever see rainbows oil makes on mud? Beautiful. Roar of gushers and people rushing in and out of the Commissary, bags full of groceries, them was boom times, strangers and newcomers, pipeline trucks stuck in Main Street bogged down in the mud, roughnecks and riggers and oilmen. Living out at Humbletown, all little gray and white company houses, that summer in Raccoon Bend the big wildcat broke through— musta been a small ocean a awl underneath us, how could we know we was all living and walking over ocean of awl under us with that much power in it to blow us to the moon?—big wildcat Hadley ⋕3 broke through and showered us all day and night and into next day with mud and rock, rocks fallin on the tin roof, windows splattered 'ith gray pastey mud and was the summer I saw my first one, 'twas astounding, 'twas shaped like a peach poutin out with a pink crease, whole little thing 'bout as big as a peach could pluck and grasp whole thing with five fingertips whole astounding thing. I was afraid

but wanted it, and Jeanette was only 'bout eight but she
started it, pulling up her dress to me. I stood her up on a
trunk and it was right before me then, all I had to do was
push, but I couldn't get it in her, tried and tried and she even
bent back and puffed it out to me, 'twas then like a whelp on
her, like something had stung her, boy I wanted to sting 'er
in that swollen whelp and I had a big stinger on me to do it
with, to sting 'er again, but I couldn't get it in her (I was
twelve). And the rushing sound of the gusher and the rocks
falling on the tin roof was an evil time. And I remember then
that the wildcat fire broke out in Sanger ♯4 and come to us
then like Satan had sent him a strange scary man named
Firedevil Prescott to put out the terrible fire. He come in his
glistening white garment with the red devil on the back, his
trademark, fireproof, like a big cottony angel, head like 'twas
all bandaged, fireproof isinglass mask for him to see through,
I was afraid to look upon him, to look him in the face, to see
his terrible face. I turned away because I was sinful, because
of what I'd done with Jeanette. I was afraid he would take me
like the Devil and throw me into the heat, and burn me in
the hellfire of Sanger ♯4; I could not look him in the face;
but those who saw his face said 'twas scary and like the
Devil's face with big yellow eyes and a horned nose; and 's
feet was all like bandaged up, big white cottony clomping
feet, like a terrible ghost's. And his glistening suit had like
tiny pieces of silver and glass and shining lights in it; and oh
my God how the flame shone and glinted blue and red and
purple and silver in that suit. He went straight into the singe-
ing fire as if it was just a lighted room where he was going to
sit down and have him some supper or visit with somebody,
not holding back, carrying a big red bottle, sausage-shaped,
and out of which came foaming white stuff upon the flames,
to quell them. For a time Firedevil Prescott was lost to us in
the fire, he had been licked up, swallowed. Once in a while
we could see the red Devil leaping and darting in the flame as
if it had got loose from Firedevil's back and had leapt into the

fire, to its very heart, and was fighting it alone. The flame turned blue then white and then a vile yellow-green that burnt our throats and then black smoke boiled and rolled out of this blackness and darkness folded over the glistening white figure of Firedevil Prescott. We waited, miserable and afraid. Firedevil Prescott had turned the bursting blinding light into sulphurous darkness; we stood choking and scared and blind in the stinking blackness, all our light and sparkling magic had vanished. And oh had the conflagration burnt him up, was he fallen down charred in that holocaust, burnt to soot? We waited in horror round the crackling flames and oh my God Lord Jesus he arose, stumbling white shape, grimy ghost out of the tarry blackness. Firedevil Prescott had survived the infernal fire and he bowed and waved, and the crowd cheered and whistled. And oh I was cryin and whistlin and wavin my arms and tears of remorse and forgiveness and thanksgiving drenched out of my eyes; and jumpin and yellin and cryin all my tears of shame and mercy, touched by grace, I vowed to myself and to God that I would never sin again like I did with Jeanette, that I would never give myself again to feelings like that, that I would be pure and without stain on myself; and the fire was quenched, the black smoke rolled away, and Firedevil Prescott was victorious.

12

The Making of
Wylie Prescott

But beware of Wylie Prescott when he would come into an area to "develop" it. "I'm going to make three million by time I'm thirty," he told people. And by God, he had, and some more. At thirty-three he had developed all the burnt-out timberland in the Thicket north of Rose, result of an accidental fire which he quenched by donning his old asbestos suit that had made him famous as "Firedevil Prescott" and going into the flames to the very heart of the fire and there fighting it at its heart as though it was Satan himself. He named it Prescott Clearing.

At twenty-two Wylie Prescott became the fabulous daredevil fighter of oilwell fires in the boom oilfields of East Texas. People came from far and near to watch the firefighter, fantastic quencher, go into the blaze and fight at the flames like a flame himself. He was the hero of the oilfields. He conquered many an oil fire and saved many an oilwell. Oilmen would pay him anything to rescue their oil; and saving millions for others, he got some for himself and so became a rich man. He emerged from the fiery depths of the golden opening in the earth that was like the throat of a large bloom that spewed forth mud, rock, salt water, and shining leathery black oil, demanding a percentage of what he had rescued. Thus he rose up out of burning holes to become a man of power and wealth, a handsome, clean-cut young man who knew exactly what he wanted. It was clear that he was going to be a leader of his fellow men. He seemed to have been born out of a molten oil hole. Having gone alone into the very throat of the golden mouth that curled out a livid tongue of gold, Wylie Prescott was initiated into the mysteries of oil and fire. He knew burning, combustion, what kindles, explodes, and bursts into blaze. So much at the very fountainhead of the natural resource of oil, he felt a primitive and mystical kinship to it; he felt as if, almost, he had created it, for he was at the source, seminal to it. Because of this mysterious alliance with oil afire, he felt somewhat divine.

Firedevil Prescott began to look for his own oil. He clawed in seeps with his fingernails after smelling oil, and behold, he pulled out oily fingers. He bought some rigging and bored his own hole in the Thicket. Oil shot up, mixed with mud and rock, and devastated an acre. Wylie rolled with joy in the oil mud. There was a fire which Wylie, in his asbestos suit with the Devil on its back, went into and calmed; this time he was saving his own oil. Already he didn't need anybody, and he was only twenty-three; he could do everything for himself. He had his secrets, his mysteries, his hunches. He would keep his mouth shut and get what was his—power, money. And he would fuck anybody who got in his way.

He became the first independent oil-well driller in East Texas. He leased land and he bought out leases. He now knew oil as he knew fire. He had gone after fire with his very hands, fondling it; he physically handled it, in hand-to-hand intimacy, like a snake handler, a broncobuster, a lion tamer, a crocodile wrestler. Now he went after oil with the same sensuality. Once in combat with a furious conflagration in Daisetta, there rose such a blast of hot gas and boiling water from some deep Hell's lake sizzling brimstone under earth, that he was blasted, ignescent, into the air, a shaft of flame. In his burning oilsoaked asbestos, his great cloudlike feet seemed to float him upright. He hung at a glowing standstill for a mo-

ment, then, winged orange flame flashing in the light like a
flaming angel out of the gray sky, he landed on a henhouse
twelve miles away. Crashing into the latticework and straw,
he set it afire, including the White Leghorns, and flaming
hens shot through the air like meteors and roosters fanned
the fire with flaming wings in the holocaust. The farmer was
aghast but came after this demon with a rake. But the demon
was fighting the very fire he'd caused and so the farmer
helped him. Wylie Prescott put out the fire and then, his suit
still burning, ran aglow into the pond, where the water burnt.
He sank in the mud to his shoulders and steam and flame sur-
rounded him. The geese and turkeys became fiendish, gar-
gling their insane sounds like the damned. The odor of burnt
egg and chickenflesh was awful.

When Wylie Prescott walked away from the burnt farm he
was ready for another kind of power. He entered the Thicket
and began to develop it. In the Thicket at first he put out
fires which were accidental fires, and with the natural clearing left by burnouts, Wylie Prescott then began his development operations. He built a log house in the clearing and offered it for sale—to anybody who wished to live in the woods,
rustic, on weekends out of the city of Houston. A whole sub-
division followed. This was the beginning of Prescott Clearing.

In Prescott Clearing, Wylie Prescott cut down green faster
than a plague of locusts. He put the Indians and Mexicans
and Negroes to work at fifty cents a day and meals—corn-
bread and Razorback pork and greens—served at a commissary set up in the Thicket. At first his crew lived in tent
camps in the woods, but soon he built shacks for the families.
Some organizers tried to get in but were driven away. One or
two were caught and cut; their parts were found hanging in
trees. Buzzards pecked at them. Wylie Prescott came to be
widely respected among the colored people. They brought
their babies to him, yellow, black and red. He had a Cushata
woman for some time and everyone knew it. Her name was

Columbia, and one day she was found floating in the log pond like an odd boat with a corncob mast sticking out of it.

Wylie Prescott tore great clumps of thick undergrowth, like hair, off the Thicket. He would go barehanded into a moist tender green overhang of willows, white hawthorn, cypress, grapevine and water oaks, and stare at it as if it were fire and then pull it all apart and root it up and get it away, mysterious life doused like green fire, until only hard dead earth remained. He quieted the raging green life of whole groves. People of Thicket border towns saw the trees coming through like corpses on wagons every day. He reached a new fury in himself—something beyond him. When he found a man cutting his magnolia saplings, he pared out his navel like the core of an apple and nailed it to a tree and wound the man around and around until he was bound to the tree by his intestines. He knew how to fell a tree—he understood growing wood and how to stop it—like a hunter knows his bird and how to bring it down, to "lower it," as Wylie put it. He was accursed with the sense of destruction, marked like Cain, by the natural gift, the ancient instinct for devastation. To bring down or dig up was his natural urge. What grew he went right to, to cut down. What ran under the earth he clawed down after and sucked it up and got it out—he wanted it *out* and in his hands; tore up everything to get down to something; and when he had got it all, turned and took it away and left a wasteland. He was a walking Plague, a pestilence, locust, frog, grasshopper, tree moth, a devourer, worse than any chemical spray or poison, a devastator. He took away from Nature its pure self, its forces, and did not put back anything, but he added fake stuff—chemicals, preservatives, coloratives. His factories murdered rivers, spoiled freshness, soured and embittered sweetness, withered green. He was the first, the leader, the beginning of the generation that poisoned itself, that spoiled its own, that ate its own poison. Wylie Prescott left a ghost forest of burnouts, sinks from salt-water overflow, slews from oilwell drillings, junk from pipeline digging. Nothing lived in his devastation. He drilled and dug and hacked and tore up the wilderness. He opened out of the earth volcanoes of salt water that spewed hundreds of feet into the air, shot off geysers of salt and slag and crude that blackened trees and vines and encrusted acre upon acre with salt cake. He created a landscape of slews and sumps.

Wylie Prescott had became a millionaire ten times over. He had taken over the lumber railroad after laying ties and tracks into the wilderness and setting up jackleg lumber mills; and in early 1940 he sold Prescott Clearing and its mill and railroad and all his oilworks and moved into the young city of Rose. Now his chemical plants on the Bay were fiery and silvered shapes of a strange, unnatural world. The looming that throbbed and quivered over the spectral Prescott Works could be seen for miles at night. It was a world of twinkling golden lights and faery silvered spires and domes that steamed and thundered and whistled, and sent a yellow fog and a vile brownish smell over the countryside that burnt eyes and soured nostrils. It curled the leaves of trees; it pockmarked granite and brick; it lay putrid over streams and bayous. Wylie Prescott was cooking and refining something. Would he get his hands on everything? He was brewing a famous dye that would enhance the color of dull-hued food or add color where there was none, and his ghostly Works were simmering and distilling the lethal mists of a chemical spray that would save crops and ruin rivers and break the chain of life. He was suspected and accused of swindling some people, of bribing others, of outright stealing from some more. Nevertheless, he got himself land along the Bays and Bayous. He developed a whole inner city with its own shopping center, banks, and even a lavish million-dollar theater for classic plays. It was in the mid-fifties when he was mentioned emphatically as a candidate for high office in state government, but he would not run. He was already building the Prescott Mansion, with parts of it coming from Belgium and Italy. Its stone and brick battlements, tentlike peaks and towers and domes were rising like a whole town over the countryside of little frame houses. In the distance farmers could see awesome winged shapes of dragons perched on leaded peaks as if just lit there with wings half-furled.

The Prescott Mansion was made of Texas blue granite, white limestone and red sandstone, but many parts of it had come from Europe by boat to Galveston, and from there on truck. Its corners rose up in four towers topped with tiled cones from Belgium. And into it came the glass tub of Mr. de Persia, bought by the decorator from an antique shop in an old barn run by two boys from Crockett who had good taste. Wylie Prescott loved the glass tub and would lie in it for hours, hoping to cure his softness, for he wanted a son to bring to the great house. There were many chimneys, imported from France, narrow Roman bricks from Italy, vases from Venice, vases from Pisa, polished marble pillars from Siena, French mirrors, clear as water, from ceiling to floor. There were mantels and fireplaces made from Numidian marble; there were arcades of Romanesque windows, colonnades and running arcades. There were massive oak doors and flowing buoyant stairways, wide and wandering staircases; glass doors; brass, copper and tile. Walls were covered with gold satin damask with gold beading and silvery satin damask with silver beading. There was white mahogany, satinwood, bird's-eye maple. The finials and lightning rods were alive with lion heads and flowers, cornucopias, winged things, shell shapes, glass rosettes and iron lilies, so that the whole topping of the great house seemed, in the fluttering dawn and trembling twilight, like some extravagant cake. There was a conservatory filled with ferns. And under this crowning roof there lived the man who had walked into fire and quenched it, who had cleared with his hands a piece of the Thicket, and dug oil with his fingernails, an odd, shut-up man who never entered any of the splendid rooms but one, a small ordinary back room under the stairs whose bottom, his ceiling, was shaped like the keel of a ship and where a picture of him in his firedevil suit glared blankly from the wall like a moonwalker.

13
Horse and
Selina Rosheen

But Wylie Prescott was tired of living alone in his mansion. He decided to search for a woman to live with him. He had had little time for serious concern with a woman, although he had found women enough to use on the run as he fled on to what the Devil on his back was driving him to—what was it? Anyway, he brought Selina Rosheen, the mysterious woman with a hidden past, to his mansion as his wife. When Wylie Prescott asked her, "Tell me about your past," she responded, "There is a gap. My past is obscured in some Hidden Years—there are no facts available, only conjecture. Take me as I am, sum total of whatever my former life adds up to, what I am right now." This excited Wylie Prescott and it appealed to him because he was a man of silence and secrets, and the delving question he put to Selina was unusual, for him. "Forget it," he said to Selina Rosheen.

Selina Rosheen had a fantastic horse named Horse, a gray, white-spotted stallion whose immense testicles hung from him like cantaloupes. In the golden days of his great fame in the Rodeo Circus, Horse was called "The Horse With Teeth of Iron," for he held on to a whirling leather strap high in the blue-lit air with what was reputed to be the strongest teeth in the world. Selina Rosheen rode, in feathers of green, astride him, waving to the crowds. But the Horse With Teeth of Iron

was the artist; and he was a beautiful sight to see. Later, when
The Horse With Teeth Of Iron was so famous, his amazing
teeth were capped and overlaid with pure gold leaf, and he
was called from then on "The Horse With Teeth Of Gold." The
Horse With Teeth Of Gold had been a beautiful thing to see as
he whirled round and round, arching his graceful body in air
like a dancer's. His tresses of pure white mane flowed like a
stream, and his delicate hooves, whose shoes were studded
with rhinestones, glittered in the pale light shed on him by a
blue spotlight. With his golden teeth gleaming, his front feet
arched forward *en pointe*, flowing head elevated in air, hind
feet extended in a graceful balletic curve, so that he looked like
some starry figure in a constellation or a flamboyant hobby-
horse, Horse froze his body in a swan-dive position, with his
great ballocks gently swaying; and time and time again, all
over the Southwest, he hushed millions beneath him, and year
after year he was named Horse of the Year. But now he was
old and had lost his teeth of gold and had to be fed a kind of
mush. To see him now was to look at nothing more than an ordinary old horse dozing his toothless head. His magic was
gone. Selina Rosheen, The Woman of the Hidden Years, fought
to keep her magic, but it was fading fast too, since she and
Horse were so bound together in enchantment. But Selina used
makeup to paint over the aging features of her face and neck
and had bright Rodeo costumes made, with tassles and sequins
and silver stars, that would bring back some of her lost magic.

It was when Horse With Teeth Of Gold fell in his frozen
swan-dive position, rump over the cannon's mouth, upon the
cannon where Jacques Devo was already balled up in it waiting to be shot off, that Horse's fantastic career plummeted.
People saw Jacques Devo fly in air bearing two large objects in
his hands, as if he were a winged god with some treasured gift
of something, of a big eggplant or something, for somebody.
The Whistling Flamingo With Wings of Coral and Pearl and
Beak of Pure Onyx, one of the spectacular features of the Rodeo Circus, waiting on his sequined perch for his act, which

was to whistle to the direction of Monsieur Phillipe's baton in silvery clear and piercing notes, "Exactly Like You," knew a pair of balls when he saw one and swiftly plunged and swiftly plucked them from Jacques Devo's hands, and with them seized in his beak of pure onyx, rose majestically to the top of the tent, like some odd creature with its sex at its throat.

The whole Rodeo Circus was in a quandary and an uproar. All Jacques Devo, safely landed in his net, could keep saying was, "What happened?" The audience was ruffling like a giant fowl, some were standing and pointing to the tent top, others were glaring with astonished eyes at a horse astride a cannon. Rodeo people were trying to get The Horse With Teeth of Gold and Selina Rosheen off the cannon, where Horse now seemed to be a suspended horse with a large black anal opening that looked like the mouth of a cannon and a ball of green feathers on his back, for Selina Rosheen was balled up and frozen with shock. A whole flight of aerialists was swarming near the tent top, rising, zooming, poking with their balancing poles, in pursuit of The Whistling Flamingo, now perched at the top of the tent, dangling heavily from his beak what looked like a pair of massive castanets. Monsieur Phillipe was bellowing over a bullhorn the cue for The Whistling Flamingo's song, but the bird would not be duped. Within another moment The Whistling Flamingo had vanished through the hole at the top of the tent on its wings of coral and pearl, carrying into the sky the superb and vaunted endowment of The Horse With Teeth of Gold. After that, Horse, who had with careful maneuvers been lifted by a belly strap on a cherry picker from Jacques Devo's cannon, suffered such a decline of spirit that his golden teeth fell out like giant seeds. Selina gathered them into a velveteen pouch which she tied around her waist and kept always there, softly clashing when she moved, as if searching for the strap of leather they once clinched.

But now Horse and Selina Rosheen had the most lavish place in the world as their home—and a lifetime friend in Wylie Prescott. At first it was thought that they would put Horse in the

Conservatory of Ferns to live. But Horse was too broken, despondent and shamed to be in a glass house, visible to the world. And so it was decided to build a special dwelling for him. Like a creature of the Parthenon, of an ancient frieze, Horse dwelt in a marble colonnaded temple under a dome of blue crystal and porcelain. There, even in his black dispiritment, in his melancholy, Horse was still of such affections and tender passions that he would assume the most heroic and sentimental stances, a horse of soul, divine elegance and the poetry of suffering. If one moment he seemed, miraculously, a rollicking, splashing creature of spray and foam in a fountain, the next he would be a horse of fury and terror rearing transcendent and apocalyptic; and then, again, a rosy gay creature of sunny meadows. But these were his visions when he was in a kind of madness, and hallucinatory, and they presaged his coming end. Most of the time he dozed all day, standing on his drab feet and dropping his toothless head, gums without their glory, meditating, no doubt, on his past days, a broken, gelded recluse with only his devoted rider, the once beautiful Selina Rosheen, to comfort him. She burnished the rhinestones with everything from pumice to chamois, but the once glittering stones would not shine again. Poor Horse.

This lugubrious situation did not enhance Selina Rosheen's assets as a wife for Wylie Prescott. But he so adored Selina that she could do no wrong. He really only wanted some life in his vast empire of a house and after a fruitless wedding night with his bride, a real nightmare, he never touched Selina Rosheen again. Selina Rosheen was relieved, since she had found Wylie's body singed of all its hair and a weblike growth of scalded skin over many parts of him, scaled like a snake's. And he had burnt breath, smelling of old fire and sulphur.

Wylie Prescott seemed to love Horse as much as he did Selina and one of the sayings about him in town was that he really married Horse. Wylie Prescott did, it must be said, give Horse, in his despair and disintegration, a comfortable and

easy life as he weakened and faded away. So that on the morning when Wylie and Selina found him a possible suicide, it was
almost as if they expected to find a note from him. Horse had
hanged himself on a bellpull of chains of gold which were
wound around his neck, and he hung in his old swan-dive
shape, shoes lusterless, mouth slack and gray, his head nevertheless held in its old arabesque as regal as in the olden days,
as if clutching with his old teeth of gold the flying strap, although his once waterfall mane stuck from his rough neck in
colorless straws and he looked like an attic rockinghorse. Wylie
Prescott apotheosized him. Horse was cast in golden bronze
with diamonds in his hooves and the purest gold for his teeth,
preserved forever in the very shape he once floated in, hanging
by his incredible teeth, and he was mounted on the topmost
spire of the mansion, an aerial being of lyric majesty, creature
of fable and fancy and dreams, immortal now.

14

The Legacy of Rose

While on a business trip to Ecuador, Selina Rosheen Prescott became the richest woman in one part of the world due to the sudden death of her husband, Wylie Prescott. An old fire wound in his lung, which only he knew about—he had swallowed a small dagger of flame in a well fire in Orange years ago—finally killed him, as though it had flared up and stabbed his heart. Selina Rosheen and an Ecuadorean doctor called to his rescue presumed it was a heart attack. But Wylie Prescott died by fire—of a burnt heart. It was said that Selina Rosheen's inheritance amounted to more than fifty millions.

Up then rose Selina as a powerful person in Texas in chemicals and dyes—something she had never dreamt of being and was not sure, at first, what to do about. She despised dyes and she hated chemicals. Wasn't there something she could convert the huge Rose Works to? The City Council, hearing rumors that she was entertaining destructive notions about the giant Prescott Industry, convened with her to persuade her to let the City be of assistance to her, but she wouldn't. They then wanted her to run for City Councilwoman, seeing the extent of her power, but she wouldn't. An ecology-minded City Commissioner implored her to install filters in the Rose Works, but she wouldn't.

Instead, what Selina Rosheen did was to take all color out of the dyes and all chemicals out of the chemicals. Mud-colored food and beverage resulted, and because of the absence of chemicals, nothing jelled or mixed or held together; and without preservatives everything spoiled and turned quickly rotten. Self-poisoned, the great vats of coloratives breathed out a putrid stench over the region, and self-ignited, the huge tanks of chemicals burst asunder, causing an earth-shaking explosion. The Rose Works afire mocked their own creator, the very Prince of Fire, Wylie Prescott, who was not alive to fight the fire that consumed his own creation.

A weird landscape for a mile around the Works resulted: the very earth was dyed. People came to the edge of it and stared. Trees looked like artificial Christmas trees sprayed pink, orange, and an ungodly puce; grass, flowers, all the fields were candy-colored. Houses and buildings had simply melted into themselves, leaving colored puffs like a confection. Multicolored ash and a peculiar kind of hideous green slag remained. No dwelling stood within a wide range of the devastation. But in the distance stood the great Mansion, a bastion in the midst of ruins.

This was in the 1950s, and already there were fourteen railroads meeting the sea from the City of Rose via a ship channel for ships from the Gulf to bring in imports and take away cotton, oil, grain, lumber. Wylie Prescott built and owned the Prescott Wharves, as he had something to do with digging the channel, and before his death he had begun plans for a shipbuilding yard, which was finished after he died. On his railroad he was already bringing in lumber from the Northwest, since he had thinned out or completely eliminated a good part of the growing wood of the Thicket.

Over what had been bayou swampland of snakes, roaches and mosquitoes, a new city, which Wylie Prescott had had a big hand in founding, was rising. In the humid lowlands the oilmen were filling in acres of standing water and planning buildings and banks and sumptuous homes. There would be Highways and Throughways and Expressways, viaducts, overpasses, Clover-leafs. Into the new city had come the small-town people whose lands, now called "lease," was leased to the oil companies, or whose little towns had been starved out by farmlands becoming mudlands or dry wastes from the oil boom.

The gigantic Rose Works sank partly into itself and partly into a strange lake created by the volcanic blast and was a curious hulked shape reflected in the water, like a humped monster; and the rest had been so melted by the molten heat, its spires twisted, its domes and cones so spun and blown by heat into delicate and graceful shapes, that it looked quite like something frozen—or that a spider might have spun.

Selina decided to preserve the fantastic ruin as a monument to itself—something which, in destroying itself created something better than it had been—self-improved. She would plant groves of trees and new grass and flowerbeds. It would be a vast park, with fresh water, protected from the hideous shopping centers and cemented land, a fortress against the advancing ugly subdivisions and discount stores. But despite her plans —and to her complete surprise—she was overcome by the City, which found some hidden clause in its laws justifying the appropriation of properties misused—even by their owner: a ridiculous local law but Selina was not of a mind to contest it further and so accepted a fat sum as compensation for what the City called Vandalism. The wreckage of Rose Works would be cleared away and something more practical, more sensible, would replace it, the City informed her. Let Selina Rosheen indulge her follies at home. Plans for a gigantic domed enclosure were announced by a rich man who bought, at once, the Works property from the City. Somebody was going to enclose and cover the largest piece of ground so captured by mankind since St. Peter's—plus aircondition it.

Well, that was Selina's first defeat. She was beginning to wish that more years in her life were hidden—namely, the present one, it was so discouraging. Was she so rich and powerful as at first it seemed? Why of course! What about the wharves, the railroad, the shipyards? Well, we'll see about that in a minute.

For there had come in haste to the Mansion a figure with traces of tar under his fingernails,—was it an old shabby angel with long white hair? Ex-Cleon Peters, old Oil King! After lying wretched in shame in his Hell of the Thicket, clawing the foul tar off his body—he now had scars to show where he flayed himself, tearing at the tar—he had regained his Faith through suffering, humiliation and rejection. He had become a new man, purged of all hatred of his enemies. And this was just as well, for whose actual house was he approaching but that of his archenemy. In the Thicket, standing under the sorrowful tree, he had heard the blast, seen the colored flames far in the distance, and thought it was the End of the World. The vision of the tragic tree was a forerunner and a prophecy! He'd been right! It had come, after all!

Now he made *his* Second Coming, running overjoyed through the landscape of the ending world toward the dazzling rockets and rainbows of bursting colored fires and the thunder that he knew to be the celestial rending of the heavens of Doomsday. He was not at all surprised at the colored fields, which he thought a bit gaudy, but if that was God's taste for the Elysian Fields then who was he, Oil King, a poor worm who'd already gone through the burning tars of Hell, and now saved, to criticize the decor of Heaven—chartreuse! . . . not what he'd envisioned but . . . O.K. When he had finally seen ahead a Heavenly Mansion, he knew he was home—Home, at last, my Savior. And at the Mansion, when the great doors of glass and gold opened—here the taste of the Heavenly Designer was first-rate—what a company was there to receive him! The beautiful Selina—an angel! And the Xylophone Twins, Hester and Esther, who had tales to tell of their escape on the terrible night of the tarring and feathering and of further adventures that befell them before they arrived, miraculously, at the Mansion. What stories they all had to tell. And Jake! Oil King could not believe his eyes and wept and wept. By means of a journey not to be believed, Jake had come to live in the Mansion in the Conservatory of Ferns. But where was the tongueless boy of the road? Alas, no one could tell Oil King, nor even knew who or what he meant. Oil King wept again, praying to God that nothing evil had overtaken Addis Adair and again realizing, as he used to, that Jake was creature and not human and so could tell him nothing. If Jake could talk, what stories he could tell! But they told Oil King how content Jake was, living in the Conservatory of Ferns casting his rubies seasonally among the cool ferns, striking out his poison from time to time—it was nature in him—he had to. And once in a while he could be heard rattling like a distant Spanish dancer.

When Oil King heard that this was not Heaven but the house of his very persecutor, Wylie Prescott, he had to use all the faith he could muster to stay—a true test and one which Jake, no doubt, had had to withstand, as well, in the beginning. For he, too, had suffered at the hands of Wylie Prescott's forces of evil. Jake, too, had had his old faith restored—and, sure enough, here was his old beloved master who had changed his life, Cleon Peters, reunited with him. What a life it had been! Who would believe what everybody had gone through.

What happened to Faithful Jake was this. In the tumult of the crowd, when Oil King was suddenly seized by his enemies, Addis had been knocked to the platform. At this moment the top of the cage had flown open and out Jake plopped like soft dough. He found himself vulnerable to a thousand heels, and only a miracle and the guidance of God steered his sliding course through the stampeding feet of humanity.

All night the fanatic hunters hunted the snake and the boy. How they despised snakes, rat-bellied bastards. In their fury they routed and killed half a hundred, but not a one was white. They hung them, heads crushed, on poles carried between their shoulders, strutting and making lewd jokes. They bedeviled nervous nests of flashing heads and stopped the dry whirring with a huge stone they dropped. Once they lashed with hot oil a hideous hole full of snakes, and the vipers, in agony, bit each other to death. One man was bitten by a huge vicious diamondback that struck like a dagger at his throat. His companions fled him in fear, for they felt that the Devil was abroad that night, skulking and darting among them in the black night; and the bitten man writhed foaming in the dirt and died in agony. It was said that his eyeballs popped out and his tongue swelled out big as an arm and broke open his mouth from ear to ear; and his liver burst through his belly.

He had been a creature of guilt because, having spoken once, he was the cause of the incessant chagrin of mankind. The responsibility of his act in that early garden was almost too much to bear. Not only had all mankind fallen, but *he* had fallen, too —cursed to the ground on his belly forever.

But the love of a wandering preacher, Cleon Peters, had taught him faith, and faith had cast out the Devil from him. The Devil no longer dwelt in Jake nor spoke through him nor used him as his tool. Cleon Peters had exorcised the Fiend and given Jake salvation. And Jake, in turn, had bestowed the Saving Grace upon Cleon Peters. And the silent love and tenderness of Addis Adair, who had purchased him for ten dollars, was a beautiful gift to any creature in its aging years.

(Now this is the way *I* look at it, the life and adventures of Jake the white rattlesnake. You may be a snake hater and disagree with me. God knows, for some of the ideas and opinions I have and have openly expressed, I could be tarred and feathered or put in the Insane Asylum up at Rusk. But I don't care. Who's telling this story, anyway; who's singing this song?)

Now Jake was a thing of such innocence, so guileless, absolutely without cunning, that he was totally open to the world and to his enemies. He just lived and moved on faith. He had become so tame and gentled, living for the most part upon the breast of mankind, that he scarcely knew creature nature any longer, so close to human nature and the ways of men had he been. But now he was alone and hunted and his life was in peril, his future very uncertain.

He came upon the white earth of the oil desert. In taking oil out of the land, men had taken all green away, had blanched the landscape as if it had been bled out. The white, caked earth camouflaged him except that his rubies looked like drops of blood on the white ground. He had little safety—on white, red; or red, white—except in darkness, and if he had to seek darkness was that what this meant, that he was thrown back into the gloom of sin and punishment? When he had been re-deemed? Wherever he would go now, men would try to kill him. The cause of Cleon Peters and sweet Addis Adair was set back centuries. He was already half Cain as he wandered and sought hiding places, hated by men, his murderers. He needed the faith of men again or he was lost. Who would give it to him?

He went on, on his belly, through the dust of the ground, over miles, through grass and marsh and meadow and prairie, rest-ing among wild flowers, hiding under stones, old ancestor. Whatever his journey was, what he encountered, the trials and sufferings he experienced, no one, of course, can fully know. But he came, at long blessed last, to the great splendid fortress and haven of Wylie Prescott's Mansion, where Wylie Prescott discovered him lying at the point of starvation and exhaustion at the edge of a lily pond, hanging over its side like some frayed rope that had been tied to something at the bottom of the pond and had rotted in two. The white rattlesnake! Wylie Prescott's memory flashed back to the day in the oilfields when Oil King had been routed out and he had seen for a moment the boy with the snake on his breast who had caused such commotion in the oilfields. "Get me that boy!" he had ordered, and left the ugly scene—which had brought him a fortune. But of course they could never find the boy. When Wylie Prescott later heard that the boy's name was Addis Adair, he burst into a rage of impatience and pounded his fist and shouted, *"Find him! Find Addis Adair!"* But nobody could find him—and anyway that was some time ago, before the mysterious change in Wylie Prescott.

Now Wylie Prescott, the peculiar millionaire who blindly destroyed and heartily salvaged, and into whose hands all things seemed to come, was overjoyed at the arrival of Jake, and he brought him into his Mansion at once and put him in the Conservatory of Ferns, where he nursed him and saved his life. (Jake's faith was thereby restored—and by Wylie Prescott!) He kept whispering to Jake, "Where is the boy? Where is Addis Adair?", as if the snake could talk. For you see, in his peculiar last years, when Wylie Prescott had had secret premonitions of his own impending death, he had begun to hope and wish for Addis to come so that he would have a male heir of more or less family blood. "He's not even your family," somebody said to him. "He's adopted. Another man's son." "Who knows what a family is? We're all adopted," is what Wylie Prescott said in his peculiar last years—a philosophy which no one truly understood. "All sons of another man," he mystically announced. Often Wylie Prescott would look out a window and say, "Maybe Addis Adair will soon come." His yearning for a distant member of his family, and not even blood kin, was unexplainable. Was his mind burnt? Had riches poisoned his judgment? Wylie Prescott was too young to have an illegitimate son as old as Addis, so that wasn't it. Had there been some secret meeting, connection, relationship between the two? Who knew? It could have been that Wylie Prescott experienced the expectation that everybody has, at one time or another in their lives—something going to return; or something going to arrive, bright and fresh and changing everything. A natural human anticipation. Except when you have about a billion dollars and are having premonitions of impending death. The Will of Wylie Prescott! Where was that and what was in it? But wait a minute.

Could it have been Selina? Did some ghost of a son haunt her, in her silence, in her colorful and attractive obscurity? Had she left a note somewhere, in a safe, or buried in the ground under a stone, or in some unknown person's sworn care who, at a certain time, would appear like a phantom or mystery person and make a startling announcement? Had she opened her mouth once and spoken of a long time ago? Did she even remember? She had lived and behaved like a person without memory, without a past life, even—as though her past life had been material evidence that had been destroyed. Her past life was not available—destroyed evidence! Ever come across anybody like that? Yet there was a remnant of her past—who has one? Had her buried life's secret come to its ironic reward? Well, you could drive yourself crazy. Still, eavesdroppers—and Selina Rosheen too—continued to hear his simple plea, "Maybe he'll come." Wylie Prescott, into whose hands all things seemed to come, could not summon into his hold Addis Adair. In the way that Mr. de Persia was once longed for by others, Addis, son of the lost restorer, made in the air and found in a log, now was longed for by Wylie. Why was this? Had Fate played a fast one on Mr. W. Prescott? Was it realized how closely in touch with the very true parentage of Addis Wylie Prescott was? For a man through whom nature worked blindly, as you have seen, and a natural saver and a natural rescuer who was moved by sheer instinct in his anticipation of Addis, and with all his money and all his ingenuity could get anything, just about, that he wanted, wasn't it sad that he couldn't recall this irrecoverable Addis Adair? He could create a living seine of hunters and searchers for Addis, send a thousand detectives over the world, send telegrams to kingdoms and governments, even have it written across the sky: *Come back Addis Adair.* Yet of all the scattered things that he had brought back together, the one thing he couldn't reassemble was a family! Almost, though. Closer than he knew. How strange life is . . . and who can understand it?

Anyway, in the Paradise Garden in the Conservatory of Ferns, old Jake cast his fading rubies among the cool fronds and lay like a lamb of pure white among the lace and feathers and curling hair of pale and deep green fern. It was a breathtaking sight—the once-accurst dweller in the drought of the ground redeemed and transfigured in the living green.

The Mansion was a living museum of vanished and salvaged things and of replicas and lifelike restorations, and, above all, some resurrections and second lives. The de Persia artifices— already antiques—had been bought by Wylie Prescott and gathered into a famous collection. The de Persia Collection was the priceless lost work of the restorer restored, though where was the lost restorer? If he could only touch the world again! There were hundreds of pieces in silver and gold, glass and iron, as you will remember him making in his old days of yore, before unusual events began to change life and the world. Even the glass tub was there, found by Wylie Prescott in an antique shop in a barn run by two boys. They'd had to cut a large hole in the Mansion roof to get it in.

Other houses rotted and fell. But Wylie Prescott had salvaged out of them—and out of the vanishing world of old Rose —the lasting beauty, the legacy of Mr. de Persia. But not Addis Adair, his most wondrous creation surpassing all others!

Upon Selina Rosheen's death, a peaceful one in which she had a death vision of Horse come for her in his old beauty and of her gliding away on Horse With Teeth Of Gold into a Blue Heaven of Paradise, Oil King became the caretaker of the Mansion, holding it all in beloved escrow until the rightful owner would come. For at Selina Rosheen's passing it came to light that the priceless Prescott properties passed into the hands of somebody who did not come forth to claim his inheritance, named Addis Adair! What had Selina known? Was she following Wylie's heart's dream and fulfilling the mysterious and fruitless call from Wylie Prescott to Addis Adair?

Would the phantom inheritor one day return to claim his legacy? The Will stipulated that the waiting period, the "period of expectation" of Addis Adair, was to be nine years and a day. The City of Rose would be responsible for holding in trust Addis Adair's inheritance until he arrived. Efforts to reach Addis Adair must be worldwide, through every kind of call and channel. Should the period of expectation be fulfilled, the Wylie Prescott fortune would go to the poor.

Would poor Oil King be once again disinherited, turned out? No one who knew him would have wanted this, but who knew this odd old man? He had so few answers to questions, knew so few facts. How had he come here to the Mansion? Via what he thought was the Second Coming, was his answer. He was not even anybody's relative. Where were the lost sweet days of Number One—with Arab and the chiming of the Xylophone and all the faithful people—days of wonder and joy before the world went bad and life turned ugly and old? He cried out, "Let me wait for Addis Adair, the boy of the road of the old days!"

Where were all his brethren, his Christian witnesses of the old days of salvation and holy glory in the Revival tents and bitterweed pastures? Would no one come forth? No one. Not even Jake, his last friend, if he could speak. Even could he speak, he wouldn't have, because he had died not long before Selina Rosheen, found by Oil King lying among the fern. He fell into a kind of ash when Oil King touched him.

And there was no time. If the City people would give him time, he'd locate his old friends in the old towns. He named towns of long ago, but they told him the towns no longer existed—they were burnt out or abandoned—white wastes. Poor Oil King. He had lost the world! This was the end for him—bitter, friendless. It was his Golgotha. It is sad to have to report that he died in the arms of a man from the City come to turn him out of the Mansion, of a failed heart. Good-bye, dear Oil King!

For a while, the empty Mansion, passed into the custody of

the City, seemed to stand in a sweet bliss of expectation, waiting for Addis Adair. Surely he would get the news. He might just come tonight, weary from a long trip; or tomorrow morning early, kicking through the dew and wiping his feet at the door. But as time passed and the expected one did not come, the homeless Mansion fell into a kind of dream, windows boarded up, dry weeds grown high around it. The City grew up rapidly around it, too, and it was pretty well ignored. The formidable income from Wylie Prescott's enterprises accumulated, waiting for Addis Adair.

Sad (and needless) to say, nine years and a day passed by and Addis Adair never arrived to claim his inheritance. There were not even any impersonators. Not even any crooked plots or schemes. And so it ended at the close of the waiting time; and on the very next day the auction began, and within two more days that was over.

Then was when the Mansion was demolished, pushed over on itself as easily as if it had been made of sand—and indeed it was a fragile structure after its precious parts had been dismantled and sold. The beauties and splendors of the Wylie Prescott Mansion were in this way scattered over a wide territory in and around Rose, and probably much farther than that —and God be with all its pieces.

And God be with you and with all the inhabitants of early Rose, now vanished, figures of sleep, death, disguise, mystery, power and beauty, whose tale I've told as best as I could recollect.

Rose flourishes, a rich and conservative city not very friendly to folly or patient with fancy, where it is not known by many that had he shown up to claim his inheritance of untold riches and glories, Addis Adair'd have been a figure of power and prestige—orphan, adopted, another's, who got closer to his very own than he ever knew, who left town and walked in mystery on the clothesline from home, among other things hidden forever were it not for my telling.

Farewell!